The Speckled Panic
&
The Choking Peril

by
Hazel Townson

Illustrated by David McKee

A Red Fox Book
Published by Random House Children's Books
20 Vauxhall Bridge Road, London SW1V 2SA
A division of Random House UK Ltd

London Melbourne Sydney Auckland
Johannesburg and agencies throughout the world

The Speckled Panic first published by Andersen Press 1982
Beaver edition 1985
Reprinted 1985 and 1989

Red Fox edition 1991

Text © Hazel Townson 1982
Illustrations © Andersen Press 1982

The Choking Peril first published by Andersen Press 1985
Beaver edition 1986
Red Fox edition 1991
Text © Hazel Townson 1985
Illustrations © Andersen Press 1986

This edition specially produced for School Book Fairs
by Red Fox 1992

Typeset by JH Graphics Ltd, Reading
Set in Linoterm Baskerville

Printed and bound in Great Britain by
Cox & Wyman Ltd, Reading, Berkshire

ISBN 0 09 922791 6

Hazel Townson

The Speckled Panic

Illustrated by David McKee

Contents

For Kenneth, who never panics

1
A Magic Purchase

One Tuesday, Kip Slater forgot to buy the toothpaste. His mother had given him a fifty-pence piece at breakfast time and asked him to fetch a tube on his way home from school.

'Make sure you don't forget, or there'll be trouble! We haven't a squeeze left in the house.'

All day Kip remembered. Then school ended and he was suddenly caught up in a very absorbing game of football. Kip arrived home at five minutes to six without the toothpaste.

Only as he was hanging up his jacket did the fifty-pence piece bounce out of his pocket and remind him of his errand. Kip groaned, chasing the coin around the hall-stand, where it finally rolled to a halt behind a boot. He picked the money up and sped off again towards the chemist's shop, never guessing that this journey was to mark a turning point in his whole life.

The chemist's shop was closed. Kip ran on towards the supermarket, but could see from half a block away that this was also closed. All the wire baskets had disappeared from the pavement outside and a man with a big bunch of keys was locking the main door. Kip groaned again. Where else could he get toothpaste at this time of day? The launderette and the fish-and-chip shop weren't much use, which left only Belle's Bazaar.

Belle's Bazaar stayed open until seven. It was a small, dim, crowded shop which sold practically everything. Belle herself was as large as the shop was small; as bright, in her colourful, gypsy-like skirts and blouses, as the shop was dim. Her big smile welcomed you, her gossip held you, but her muddle-headedness finally drove you away.

Kip leapt down the two stone steps, past the loudly-pinging doorbell and into the shadowy Bazaar. Surely somewhere, among all these balls of wool and nappy-pins and tins and cardboard boxes, there was one little tube of toothpaste, with fluoride or without?

'Now then, sonny, what can I get you?'

'Toothpaste, please!' Kip sounded desperate.

'I've only the Purple Speckled. Extra special. Very good stuff, so I'm told.'

Kip could hardly believe his luck.

Grabbing the carton that Belle held out, he quickly paid and escaped before she could change her mind. Belle called something after him, but he didn't stop to hear what it was. He was already late for tea and very hungry. Kip ran all the way home.

Only as he handed the carton over to his

mother in the brightly-lit kitchen did Kip glimpse the flowing, red script on the front of it.

'VENGER'S PURPLE SPECKLED TRUTHPASTE' it said. Or seemed to say.

Not toothpaste, but truthpaste!

It couldn't be that really, of course. It must be just a trick of the eyes, coming in from the dusk to the light.

'What sort's this supposed to be?' asked Mrs Slater. 'Purple Speckled? Never heard of it! Whatever will they think of next?'

'Let's see?'

Kip's dad looked up from his evening paper.

'*I* don't know!' he exclaimed with disgust.

'They give you strawberry flavour and green stripes and rum-and-raisin and I don't know what. Why can't we have honest-to-goodness toothpaste with no fancy gimmicks? They don't do you any good, you know, all these jazzy colourings. You may as well try and clean your teeth with a slice of blackberry tart.'

'Yes, Dad,' replied Mrs Slater patiently. 'I expect it was the name that took Kip's fancy. Caught his imagination, didn't it, son?'

Mrs Slater had not named her son Kipling for nothing.

Kip said nothing. He was concentrating on his sausage-pie-and-beans.

Mrs Slater, who carefully cleaned her teeth after every meal, but had long since despaired of ever getting Kip or his father to do likewise, bore off the Purple Speckled as soon as the meal was over. She was still in the bathroom, brushing her teeth, when a knock sounded at the front door.

Mr Slater tutted, guessing who it was. The door flew open and in walked the Slaters' next-door neighbour, fat, noisy, untidy Mrs Madding.

'Anybody home?' Mrs Madding called in an over-cheerful voice which set Mr Slater groaning. He couldn't stand Mrs Madding, and could only marvel at the patient, long-suffering way in which his wife put up with her.

'Anybody in?' Mrs Madding called again.

Mr Slater would have liked to say, 'No!' but of

course he didn't, and Mrs Madding advanced into the hall, waving an empty teacup in the air.

'Just doing a bit of baking,' she explained, poking her head round the kitchen door. 'Ran out of flour, and of course the shops are shut now. Wondered if I could borrow a cupful off you till tomorrow? I'll bring it back in the morning.'

There was a rushing sound upstairs, and before Kip or his dad could reply to Mrs Madding, Kip's mother appeared on the staircase, flourishing her toothbrush.

'Oh no, you won't fetch it back!' she cried angrily. 'You never do! We're sick and tired of lending you things. What about my egg-whisk, and Mr Slater's screw-driver, and that two pounds of sugar, and the light-bulbs and washing-powder and turpentine and our best deck-chair? We'll never see any of those again. Never! So this time you can jolly-well go and borrow your flour from somebody else!'

Well!

What a way to talk to a next-door neighbour!

What rudeness, what an unspeakable mouthful of truth!

'Here, Elsie, steady on!' muttered Mr Slater awkwardly, advancing from the kitchen.

Mrs Slater was just as horrified as Mrs Madding. For a few dramatic seconds the two women stood staring at each other, Kip's mother with a hand over her offending mouth

and Mrs Madding with the cup clenched to her bosom in shock.

Mrs Slater wanted to call out, 'Oh dear! I'm sorry!' but she found she could not. Her voice seemed to have frozen in her throat and the only sound that emerged was a croak like cracking ice.

For once in her life, Mrs Madding was utterly at a loss for words. She turned and went, slamming the door behind her. A vase on the hall table wobbled alarmingly.

Now there would be trouble! Now there'd be a street feud worse than the Wars of the Roses! Mrs Slater already dreaded the scenes she knew would follow, yet at the same time she felt glad, relieved, even light-hearted because something had been said that needed saying. Mrs Madding *was* a nuisance, always borrowing things and not returning them. Perhaps now she would stop doing it.

'Hey, Mum, that was great!' cried Kip at last.

'I don't know what came over me!' breathed Mrs Slater faintly. 'I must have gone mad!'

'Come to your senses, more like,' grinned Mr Slater. 'It's not like you to speak out, love, but you only told the truth after all.'

The truth!

Kip had a thought. 'Mum, did you just clean your teeth with that new toothpaste?'

'Yes, I did,' admitted Mrs Slater ruefully. 'And now I ought to go and wash my mouth out with soap and water. That's what I'd tell you to do if you were so rude.'

Kip suddenly bounded up the staircase, heading for the bathroom. He grabbed the toothpaste carton and studied the writing. Just as he had thought! It did say, 'VENGER'S PURPLE SPECKLED TRUTHPASTE', and the small print underneath read: 'Guaranteed to make you tell the truth for twenty-four hours after use.'

Glory be! What a find! What marvellous, incredible stuff! This was too good to waste on the family. This was a product to be cherished, to have serious fun with at school.

Thrusting the Purple Speckled into his pocket, Kip bolted downstairs again and grabbed his jacket.

'Just going round to Herbie's for a bit!'

'Well, don't forget about your homework!' Kip's dad called after him.

'Not likely!' lied Kip, running off. Just wait until that genius, Herbie Coswell, wrapped his mind round this!

2
Trial Run

Herbie Coswell's young sister Ethel had just swallowed a button. Her mother was thumping her furiously on the back when Kip arrived, and Ethel's frantic struggles were alarming.

Herbie, arms folded, stood watching thoughtfully.

'Turn her upside down,' he suggested at last.

Obediently, Mrs Coswell grabbed Ethel round the waist and swung the child's legs into the air. The button shot out of Ethel's mouth into a dish of green jelly.

'Gosh!' cried Kip admiringly. It was typical of Herbie to stand back calmly and suggest the perfect, the only possible, solution. For Herbie Coswell was a genius. His brain usually reached the finishing-post whilst everybody else's brains were under starter's orders.

Ethel began to yell. The noise was terrible.

'Oh, come on!' said Herbie in disgust. 'We'll go upstairs for some peace and quiet.'

He and Kip marched off to Herbie's bedroom.

'Kids!' Herbie flopped wearily on to the bed. 'Kids under six shouldn't be allowed to live with

16

us older folks. There should be special colonies, or something.'

'Cheer up!' Kip produced the Purple Speckled. 'I've something to show you.'

'Toothpaste? You gone mad, or something?' Herbie took the package and glanced at the writing on it. Then he sat up and glanced again.

'You've been down to the joke shop!'

'No, I haven't! It's real!'

'Makes you tell the truth? Go on, you've been had! Only torturers and psychiatrists can make you tell the truth.'

'It worked on my mum.' Kip began the tale of Mrs Madding's visit.

'That doesn't · prove anything,' scoffed Herbie. 'Your mum was just in a rotten mood.'

'No, she wasn't. My mum doesn't have rotten moods. At least, not all of a sudden, like that.'

'She got fed up with old Madding at last, and no wonder. It was a coincidence that she did it then, when she'd just cleaned her teeth.'

Kip looked crestfallen.

'Mind you,' said Herbie, reconsidering, 'I once read a book about this truth drug that they sprayed over your mouth with a watering-can . . .'

At that moment, Mrs Coswell called upstairs: 'Herbert! Just you come down here this minute!'

Now, Kip and Herbie knew that if Mrs Coswell called her son Herbert there was trouble in the offing. The boys looked at each other warily, whilst down below young Ethel went on yelling.

'What've you done now?'

'Nothing! I've been good as gold for the last half-hour.'

'Herbert, I'm waiting!' Mrs Coswell sounded like a headsman with his axe at the ready.

Herbie dragged Kip after him to face his mother in the hall.

'Herbert Coswell, you made our Ethel put that button in her mouth. You told her it was a toffee, didn't you?'

'I never!' Herbie was outraged.

'It was a wicked, irresponsible thing to do, and when your dad gets to know . . .'

'Cross my heart, Mum, I'd never do a thing like that. She might have choked for real.'

'Well, Ethel says you did.'

Herbie turned pink. 'Yeah, she would say that. She loves getting me into trouble, and you always believe her, don't you?'

'I can recognize the truth when I hear it!'

It was the mention of truth that gave Herbie his second inspiration of the evening. He signalled to Kip, who had already read Herbie's mind.

Grabbing Ethel by the hand, Kip dragged her to the bathroom whilst Herbie and his mum continued their argument.

'See the nice purple speckles,' coaxed Kip, squeezing some of the paste on to Ethel's Noddy brush. But Ethel was not in a co-operative mood. She had no intention of cleaning her teeth.

Kip fished in the depths of his pocket and found a plastic canoe from a cornflake packet.

'Brush your teeth and you can have this.'

'Don't want it!'

Kip fished in his pocket again, wondering why Herbie hadn't stuffed a whole boxful of

buttons into Ethel's sulky mouth. He came up
with a green elastic band, but Ethel didn't want
that, either. All that was left, apart from bits of
chewed string and bubble-gum, was his grubby
handkerchief. He dragged out that disgusting
object and regarded it with reverence.

'See that hanky? That used to belong to the
Emperor of Japan, that did. He lent it to my
grandad, then told him he could keep it. I can't
give it you because it's a family heirloom, but
you can look at it.'

Ethel stopped crying. She decided she wanted
the Japanese Emperor's hanky more than

anything else in the world, and made a grab for it. Kip stepped deftly aside. Ethel grabbed again, and at last the deal was made. Obediently, if messily, Ethel began to brush her teeth.

A few minutes later, Kip was able to give the thumbs-up sign to Herbie, whereupon Herbie persuaded his mum to ask Ethel again whether he had made her eat the button.

'No,' replied Ethel meekly. 'Herbie told me not to put the button in my mouth in case I swallowed it.'

Well, after that, young Ethel was sent supperless to bed, and Herbie's mum made a pile of beef-and-pickle sandwiches and a jug of lemonade for the boys to bear off triumphantly to Herbie's room.

'Now do you believe me? Does it make you tell the truth, or doesn't it?'

'Well, I must admit that wasn't a bad performance. But now you've proved your point, we're not going to waste this stuff on family squabbles.'

''Course not! Why do you think I pinched it from home?'

'We must think,' said Herbie solemnly, 'how best to use this amazing product for the benefit of mankind.'

For a quarter of an hour they did sit and think, the silence broken only by the crunch of pickles and the slurp of lemonade. Then Herbie the

genius cried: 'Politicians! Be a nice change if *they* told the truth! We'll start with our own local MP, and work our way up to the Prime Minister.'

'Super!'

There was a pause, then Kip added: 'How will we get them to clean their teeth with this stuff, though? It was hard enough persuading your Ethel.'

'There are ways and means,' said Herbie, annoyed at being criticized.

'We can't go up to MPs in the street and ask them to start brushing their teeth.'

''Course not. We'll get the paste on to their teeth another way.'

'Such as?'

22

'We'll put it in a cake! It would go nicely in a plain sponge, with a dollop of jam to take the taste away. Blackberry jam, to cover up the purple speckles.'

'Herbie, you're a genius!' Kip told his friend admiringly. But of course Herbie Coswell knew that already.

3
The Wrong Victim

In a few days it would be Speech Day at school, and this year the prizes were to be presented by the local Member of Parliament, Cedric Clodd, an old boy of the school. Cedric did not appear often in his constituency, so when he did, no time was left to waste. He fitted in as many engagements as possible. On the evening of Speech Day, he was also to address the public in St Bede's Church Hall, to answer any questions the voters might care to put to him.

'That's when he's going to tell the truth,' cried Herbie, 'if we die in the attempt.'

Kip and Herbie knew that after the great, long, boring Speech Day ceremony there would be light refreshments for the Guest of Honour, served in the Headmaster's study. This would be a great opportunity for the boys to slip in the Truthpaste cake among the other goodies. Then they would go to the evening's political meeting and watch the fun.

'Oh, boy!' cried Kip. 'I can hardly wait. My mum's going to ask old Clodd all sorts of questions. She wants to know why the price of school dinners has gone up again, and who put the bus stop in front of my gran's garden gate.'

The two boys carefully laid their plans. If they had spent half as much time on their homework, they would have had Oxford scholarships by the tender age of twelve.

First they bought the sponge cake, which Herbie sliced lop-sidedly across the middle with his penknife. Then they spread the bottom piece with jam sneaked from Mrs Slater's larder.

Next, they squeezed some of the Truthpaste over the jam, flattening it down with a lolly-stick. When the cake was ready they put it in an old shortbread tin in which Herbie had once kept caterpillars. Then they took the tin to school and hid it in Herbie's desk.

'How can we be sure old Clodd will eat some of the cake?' Kip wondered.

'Cedric Clodd won't refuse a wedge of cream cake,' replied Herbie with confidence. 'You know how fat he is. My dad says he's just plain greedy. Anyway, after that boring afternoon he'll be ravenous. He'll probably scoff three pieces at least.'

'It's a good job the Head never touches cake. Him and his blooming crispbread and raw carrots!'

The next problem was how to get the cake into the Headmaster's study at the proper time. This was where Fate took a hand. On the morning of Speech Day their form-master asked for two volunteers to help carry the tea things from the kitchen to the Headmaster's study. Kip and Herbie managed to get themselves chosen for this enviable task, but even then their troubles were not over. Their every move was watched with dark suspicion by Mrs Emmett, the Domestic Science teacher, who accompanied them back and forth along the corridors with tray-loads of crockery, dainty sandwiches, biscuits and jam tarts. The look in Mrs

Emmett's eye proclaimed that she had counted every crumb and teaspoon and would know at once if one went missing.

It was lucky for the boys that Mrs Emmett was also in charge of first aid. Somebody had a fall in the gymnasium and Mrs Emmett was suddenly called away.

'Fine time to have an accident!' she tutted, not happy at leaving two hungry, growing boys with all that food. But of course she had to go.

'Quick! Now's our chance!'

Herbie raced for the tin. Kip rapidly divided the cake into eight, and was just dusting away the crumbs when in walked the Headmaster himself, George Dykes, MA.

Mr Dykes was in a good mood. He enjoyed Speech Day. He loved showing off in his best suit, and he enjoyed the tea-party in his study afterwards. It had become something of an occasion.

As he walked into his study now, carrying a begonia plant for the party table, Mr Dykes was positively sparkling with happy excitement.

'My word, that's a fine spread!' he exclaimed. 'You've done a good job there, Slater and Coswell! In fact, I think you've earned a small reward. Here, try some of this!'

Mr Dykes picked up the plate of Truthpaste cake and handed it to Herbie.

Herbie was shocked. 'Oh – er – thank you,

sir, but it's nearly dinner-time.' He managed a sickly grin. 'Stew today, sir. Don't want to lose my appetite.'

'Your self-control does you credit, Coswell, but I've never known a boy yet who couldn't make room for an extra piece of cake. Go on, now, take one.'

Groaning inwardly, Herbie was forced to obey.

'Now you, Slater.'

'N-no thank you, sir, really. There might not be enough to go round this afternoon.'

'Nonsense, boy, there's enough food here to feed a rugby team.'

'But – it will spoil the look of the cake if there are two pieces missing.'

'I never heard such rubbish!' cried Mr Dykes jovially. 'Anybody would think you'd just stuffed that cake with poison! Hurry up, now, or the bell will go.'

Kip, too, was compelled to accept the Headmaster's well-meaning offer.

'Well, go on, eat it! I suppose you're shy at standing there eating in front of me, is that it? All right then, I'll have a piece with you. I don't usually eat cake, but just this once. It certainly looks delicious.'

Herbie, having taken the first careful bite, avoiding the Truthpaste filling, nearly choked.

'I wouldn't if I were you, sir. It's a bit peculiar, actually.'

'Peculiar? Then I must certainly try it before I offer it to my guest. Can't give peculiar cake to our Member of Parliament, eh? Might bring the government down!'

The Headmaster took a massive bite from his piece of cake and Kip almost groaned aloud.

'H'm!' remarked the Headmaster, chewing heartily. 'It's certainly different! Very nice. Sticks to your teeth a bit, that's all.' In two more expert bites Mr Dykes finished his portion and sucked a stray blob of jam from his finger.

'Come on, boys! Eat up! Time you were off back to your classes.'

Herbie had stuffed a lump of cake into the top of each sock and was now busily chewing nothingness. As for Kip, he had sidled towards the wastepaper basket and managed to drop his cake into it unnoticed.

'You know, Slater,' Mr Dykes said suddenly, 'I've always wondered why your parents called you Kipling. Such a strange first name for a boy. Your family's not related to the author, I suppose?'

'Oh, no sir! My mum just fancied it, I think.'

'How thoughtless! The other boys must tease you unmercifully. Might have ruined your whole school career for you, a name like that.'

'Oh, I don't mind, sir. It could have been worse. She could have picked on Mowgli.'

'Really!' Mr Dykes sounded quite exasperated. 'I do think parents ought to consider this matter of names more carefully. It was selfish, foolish and short-sighted to say the least . . .'

The Headmaster's telephone began to ring, and the two boys thankfully made their escape.

'Phew! We're really in trouble now!' gasped Herbie. 'All that about your name was the hidden truth coming out, like it did with your mum and Mrs Madding. Goodness only knows what he'll say on the platform this afternoon.'

'No need to worry about that. He writes his speech out and keeps looking at his notes.'

'Suppose what he's written is just polite lies?

He won't be able to say it. Anything could happen!'

'You mean – he might say rude things about Cedric Clodd, or the governors or somebody? Oh, he wouldn't dare!'

'He just said rude things about your mother.'

'Yeah, I suppose he did.'

Herbie looked thoughtful. 'Perhaps we ought to kidnap him or something. Hide him somewhere until the truth wears off.'

4
The Chase

Anyone who has ever tried to kidnap a Headmaster will know that it is not an easy matter.
Although Kip and Herbie racked their brains all
through the rest of morning lessons, they got
nowhere. The best thing they could think of was
an urgent telephone call which would remove
Mr Dykes from the scene. But what sort of call?
Had he a mother who might be ill? A sister who
might suddenly elope with a penniless actor?
They could not tell, for Mr Dykes was a bachelor
whose family background remained a secret.
That left business. Could he be summoned to a
Headmasters' Conference in Brighton? Or to see
the Minister of Education? Or to meet a school
inspector arriving from London? All these suggestions, the boys decided, lacked the ring of
truth. Mr Dykes would immediately check.

'What then?' Kip asked wearily as the dinner-
bell sounded.

'We could own up. He might let the Deputy
Head take over.'

'Own up – and risk getting expelled or something? Not likely!'

'Well then, we can find a cure. That's the only chance left.'

'A CURE?'

'You said you bought that stuff at Belle's Bazaar. Maybe she can help us. We'll go now. We've only about two and a half hours before Speech Day assembly, so we'll have to move fast.'

'But what about our dinner?'

'Miss it, of course. There are more important things than food.'

Kip was not sure he agreed with this, but he had not time to argue, as Herbie was already dragging him away. The boys managed to slip out of school unnoticed. They crossed the playing-fields, dived through a hole in the fence and ran all the way into town.

Madame Belle had her coat on, and was turning round the card on the glass door to read CLOSED instead of OPEN. It was her lunch-time, too.

'Don't go!' yelled Herbie, banging on the glass.

Belle hesitated, then decided to open the door.

'Be quick, then!' She let them into the shop. 'Not eating today, boys? Saved your dinner money to buy something more lasting, maybe? Penknife, compass, stamp album . . .?'

The boys dived straight into their Truthpaste story.

'Oh, that!' Belle remembered the carton. 'It

was a sample I had from a traveller. Not meant
for sale really. I was going to try it out myself,
but you were in such a state that night, I gave it
you.'

Kip groaned. 'Which traveller left it?'

'Well, I don't really know, dear. He was new,
you see. Ever such a nice little redhead, but he
hadn't been here before. Still, he must have left a
card. Let's see if we can find it.'

Belle took from a drawer a bundle of little
cards printed with salesmen's names and

addresses. Agonizingly slowly, she sorted through them until at last she came up with a green one.

'Here it is!'

Both boys craned forward and were able to read, in bold, black lettering:

A. VENGER. CURES, COSMETICS, CLEANING PRODUCTS.

TELEPHONE 4988.

'Venger's Purple Speckled!' cried Kip. 'It's the same name! He must make the stuff himself. We've got to find him.'

'Come on, we'll ring him up.'

There was a telephone box round the corner, but no reply from the number on the card. Kip began hunting through the Vs in the directory to find an address.

'Venables, Venet, Venetian Blinds Ltd, Venner, Venning . . . not a Venger in sight.'

'He must be ex-directory.'

'That settles it. We'll just have to go back and own up.'

'Suppose so.'

Gloomily, the boys began to move away in the direction of school. Then suddenly, Herbie gripped Kip's arm.

'There he is, across the road! Little redhead with a suitcase showing initials A.V.!'

'Talk about luck!'

The two boys rushed across the road, risking death or maiming as they wove recklessly through the traffic. Pedestrians gasped and motorists honked their horns.

'Hey, wait!'

'Mr Venger! Just a minute!'

But the little redhead had not heard them. He walked fast along the pavement, head down, shoulders slightly hunched, eyes on the ground. He was deep in thought. Before the boys could catch him up, Mr Venger reached a bright red mini, and took a bunch of keys from his pocket.

'Stop! Wait for us!'

It was too late. The mini drew away from the pavement as they reached it.

'Huh! Some luck that turned out to be!'

'It's okay. Venger's a traveller making calls. He'll stop again soon. All we have to do is catch him up.'

They flew along the High Street in the direction the red mini had taken. Cargrove's factory was emptying for the lunch-hour and there seemed to be millions of people on the pavements, most of them intent on bumping into Kip and Herbie. Hot, bruised and breathless, they battled on for quite a distance, then Herbie, glancing up a side-street, saw the mini again, parked outside a house.

'Told you!' cried Herbie triumphantly.

'Car's empty.'

'Can't be far away. Let's look in the car for clues.'

They crossed to the mini and pressed their

noses against the glass. Kip could see a tartan rug. Was that a clue? Maybe Venger was bound for Scotland. Herbie spotted a half-eaten bag of caramels.

'He might have gone to the dentist's.'

Suddenly Kip felt a hand on his shoulder.

'Now then, what's going on here, eh?' Kip looked up into the face of a policeman.

'This your dad's car, then?' asked the policeman, keeping a tight grip on Kip and reaching out for Herbie, too.

'Er – no, we were just – looking.'

'Looking for what?'

'Clues. We wondered where the driver had gone.'

'Tried the door, did you?'

'No!' Herbie was indignant.

'Well, that's how it looked to me. Very serious offence, breaking into parked cars. Could get you into a lot of trouble.'

'Honest, we were only looking.'

'Anyway, shouldn't you be at school? I thought you young 'uns from St Bede's weren't allowed out in the dinner-hour.'

'We're doing a special errand.'

'Yes, something for Speech Day.'

'Speech Day today, is it? Then you'd better get back to school quick. Come on!'

In the iron grip of the policeman, Kip and Herbie were obliged to start walking away from the mini.

38

'Like a lift back to school?'

The policeman indicated his own car, parked across the road.

'Oh, no thanks!' Kip could just imagine the Headmaster's face if they rolled up to school in a police car after being out of bounds.

'We can walk there in five minutes.'

'Well, see that you do! Straight down this High Street and no turning back. I shall be watching you all the way.'

Releasing his grip at last, the policeman gave the boys a couple of gentle pushes to start them on their way. Kip and Herbie began walking.

Neither boy dared turn round. Maybe the

policeman was following them. On and on they walked. Only when the police car drove past them at last did they stop, watch it disappear, then turn and double back towards the red mini.

The car had gone.

'Of all the rotten luck!'

'That's *your* fault, overdoing things as usual,' grumbled Herbie.

'I like that! Whose idea was it to peer into the car in the first place?'

'Well, all right then, you come up with a better idea.'

'I will! Let's have some lunch,' replied Kip, indicating the Snowball Snack Bar a couple of doors away.

'Lunch? Is that all you can thing about?'

'Well, we aren't going to catch old Venger. We may as well go back to school and own up, and I'd do that a lot better with a snack inside me. We've missed our school dinner now.'

Reluctantly, Herbie realized how hungry he was.

'I suppose a quick sandwich wouldn't do any harm.'

They wandered into the snack bar. Kip handed some money to Herbie.

'Get me one egg-and-cress and a rock bun. I'll find us some seats.'

The snack bar was crowded with midday customers, and a pall of cigarette smoke hung gloomily round the yellow plastic lampshades.

40

Kip made his way to a far corner and flopped into the only empty chair he could see. All that excitement had sapped his strength. He ate a couple of sugar-lumps for immediate sustenance, then noticed someone leaving. He leapt up to grab the chair for Herbie. Only as he dragged it back to the table did he notice that the person at the very next table, eating hungrily away behind a propped-up newspaper, was none other than A. Venger himself.

5
Mischief with the Mustard

Herbie came struggling along with a tray. Before he reached the table, Kip started pulling faces. Herbie failed to get the message, and Kip actually had to take hold of Herbie's ear and swivel the lad's head in the right direction before the penny dropped.

'Glory be!' Herbie could hardly believe his eyes.

'Well, go on, you're nearest! Ask him for the cure!'

Herbie plonked down the tray. 'Suppose he won't tell us? It's his secret, after all. You wouldn't go blabbing your secrets to all and sundry, would you?'

'You mean, he could stuff us up with any old tale?'

Herbie bit confidently into his sandwich. 'Not if we catch him in his own trap. Get the Truthpaste out.'

Herbie then leaned across to Mr Venger's table and asked if he might borrow the mustard. The little redhead looked up from his newspaper. Two very bright blue eyes stared curiously at Herbie. Then Mr Venger handed over the mustard before turning back to his newspaper and his soup.

'Right!' hissed Herbie. 'Squeeze some Truthpaste into that mustard, quick!'

When he had finished his soup, Mr Venger exchanged the bowl for a plate of sausage-and-chips already waiting at his elbow, and began to tuck in again, still reading his newspaper.

Kip stirred the mustard vigorously with its little spoon, so that the purple Truthpaste speckles were hidden and the stuff took on a more mustard-coloured hue. Then he handed the pot to Herbie, who in turn reached over and passed it back to Mr Venger.

'Thanks! Best mustard I ever tasted!'

There was an anxious moment while Mr Venger continued eating. Perhaps he didn't like mustard. What a pity if they'd wasted all that Truthpaste! But the boys need not have worried, for Mr Venger began to spoon out quite large dollops of mustard, which he flicked on top of his sausages. Then he spread the mustard evenly with the tip of his knife, cut off a piece of sausage and ate it.

'Now for it!' breathed Herbie excitedly. He had actually leaned an arm on Venger's table, ready to pose the all-important question, when the coughing fit began.

44

Mr Venger flailed helplessly about in the grip of a sudden and terrible cough. His cheeks grew red, his eyes streamed, he groped wildly at the edge of the cloth and pulled it half off the table. Crockery slid to the floor.

Diners turned round in concern. Someone thumped Venger smartly on the back, and someone else tried to offer him a glass of water. Kip and Herbie were appalled. What had they done? The Truthpaste hadn't had this effect on anybody else. Perhaps it was just a bit of sausage gone down the wrong way, but even that made them feel guilty.

Retribution was at hand, in the shape of a plump, cross waitress who bore down upon the boys, shouting angrily: 'Hey, you two! I saw you, messing about with the gentleman's mustard-pot. What you up to, eh?'

'We were only . . .' Kip began, but the waitress had no intention of listening to excuses.

'Out!' she cried mightily, heaving Kip to his feet and Herbie after him. Before they knew it, the boys were at the door of the snack bar, clutching their rock-buns and protesting in vain. The waitress opened the door and pushed them through it.

'Kids ain't supposed to come in here without an adult, anyway!'

As she spoke, a dark blue figure loomed up

in front of the boys. It was the policeman who had moved them on from the red mini.

'Well, well! Looks like I shall have to give you that lift back to school after all. Forgotten the way, have you?'

6
The Truth about Truth

The boys were saved by Mr Venger himself, who dashed out of the snack bar, eyes still streaming, cheeks still red.

'Just a minute, Officer!' croaked the redhead, waving his handkerchief. He was only just in time. Kip was already on the back seat of the police car with Herbie being bundled in beside him. The policeman turned, and Mr Venger began to explain that he wanted to talk to the boys.

'It could be a matter of life and death.'

'Oh?' Now the policeman was really interested, but Mr Venger hastened to say that he needn't concern himself.

'Just a private matter.'

'All the same, these lads aren't supposed to be out of school.'

'You're absolutely right, Officer. I'm just going to take them back there. No need for you to trouble.'

Thankfully, Herbie backed nimbly out of the car.

'Now then!' began Mr Venger sternly when

the boys were seated in his own car. 'You've a lot of explaining to do.'

Mr Venger knew his own Truthpaste when he tasted it. What he could not understand was how these two boys had got hold of it. It seemed he had a crisis on his hands.

Arthur Venger, it must be pointed out, was no mere salesman, but a genuine artist, a man of original ideas, the actual creator of the goods he sold. In fact, Arthur thought of himself as a crusader. He had once looked up the word 'crusade' in the dictionary and it had said, 'an enterprise against some public evil'. Now, as far as Arthur could see, there were so many public evils that he scarcely knew where to begin. Litter was one, and he was at present engaged upon a cure for litter-dropping. Telling lies was another, and his Truthpaste had been, at one stage, his favourite invention. He remembered vividly the day when that particular recipe had turned out right at last. He had brushed his teeth with the Truthpaste and tried to say, 'Another failure!' only to find that he could not. All that emerged from his throat was a croak like cracking ice. For 'Another failure!' would have been a lie. The experiment had succeeded.

Yet success was not so simple. This was one experiment which Arthur soon wished he had never started.

'Well? I'm waiting to hear your story.'

Herbie nudged Kip and Kip began the tale.

49

As he listened, Arthur Venger could scarcely believe his ears.

'Are you saying that tube of Truthpaste was on sale in a shop? But it can't have been! I decided to destroy it all. Except for one sample tube, that is. I always keep one of everything I make, just for reference.'

'Destroy it all?' Herbie was horrified. 'But it's great stuff! Can't you sell it? Surely it's worth a fortune.'

Arthur Venger shook his head sadly.

'Truth's a terrible thing, as I soon discovered.'

He had made the stuff, he said, in all good faith. He had worked hard on his recipe, thinking only of what a better world it would be when lies disappeared for ever. Yet when he had tried out the stuff, he had soon found there was more to the business of truth than he had thought.

'That Truthpaste turned out to be downright dangerous. So I altered my recipe to make ordinary toothpaste instead.'

'Dangerous?' Kip echoed fearfully.

'Yes, indeed! I'll tell you a few home truths about truth. You can tell it and nobody believes you, which is enough to drive you frantic. Or you can try hard not to tell it in case you hurt somebody's feelings. Or you can think you're telling it when you're not. Or you can tell it with the best intentions and cause a whole lot of trouble. That's only the beginning. Just you think about it for a while and you'll end up with a list of complications as long as a cold, wet Sunday.'

'You mean to say it's all right to go around telling lies, then?'

'No, no; I mean there are moments when it's not wise to tell the blunt, straightforward truth. You could break somebody's heart, or make an enemy for life, or even start a war.'

'He's right, Herbie! Look at all the trouble that Truthpaste has caused since we got hold of it. First my mum's outburst, then your Ethel

51

getting sent to bed, then Mr Dykes eating that cake when he wasn't supposed to . . .'

Mr Vengar began to look alarmed. 'Who's Mr Dykes? *He* hasn't tried any Truthpaste, has he?'

'Well, as a matter of fact . . .'

Arthur began to groan as the story continued.

'Why, the man might say anything! And Speech Day on top of it all! A public audience and newspaper reporters! We must do something right away!'

'Now you're talking!' said Herbie.

'How much time have we got?'

'Oh, Speech Day's a long, boring business. Before Mr Dykes gets going there's the orchestra and the school song and that. Then the Chairman of the Governers drones on for ages, and the choir does its madrigals and stuff. We've a good bit of time yet.'

'We'll need it!' said Arthur grimly, letting in the clutch and roaring noisily away.

7
One Green Bottle

Arthur Venger lived outside the town, in a remote little bungalow, littered with ingredients, samples and dirty pots and pans. It was just as well that Arthur lived alone.

When he and the boys reached the house, Arthur rushed at once into the kitchen and unlocked the door of a cupboard marked 'EXPERIMENTAL ONLY'. Inside there were four shelves filled with bottles, jars and packages of various shapes and sizes. Arthur began to shuffle these about with growing anxiety, searching for one particular package. It was not there. Something else was there, though, which should not have been: an ordinary tube of toothpaste made from Arthur's own recipe, no longer at the EXPERIMENTAL ONLY stage. There had been a mix-up!

The little salesman took out a ledger in which he entered his shop visits. He ran his finger down a column of names and stopped at Belle's Bazaar.

'You're right! I left it there by mistake. How careless! I'm as good as a criminal, I am!'

For a moment, Arthur stood horrified. Then he pulled himself together.

'No use moaning. What we have to do is make a cure. You'll have to help me, or we'll never finish in time. Do as I say, and be very careful. Check everything twice over, to make sure you've got it right.'

As he spoke, Arthur Venger began to fill a huge pan with water, which he set on the stove to boil.

'Here are the scales. Weight 50 grams of this blue stuff and 25 grams of the green.'

Delighted to be helping, the boys obeyed.

'And when you've done that, chop these leaves up as fine as you can, then scatter them on the boiling water.'

The little kitchen began to fill with steam and peculiar odours. It took them well over an hour to produce a bottle of dark green liquid which Arthur held up to the light and studied intently. He shook the bottle, watching the colour cloud over. He sniffed it thoughtfully. Then he poured a few drops into the bottom of a glass, dipped his finger into the glass, then touched that finger to the tip of his tongue.

'H'm!' He frowned and kept silent for a minute, then his tone suddenly changed.

'Right, that'll do! I'll just lock you two boys in the cellar, then drive off to school with this cure for your Mr Dykes.'

'You'll WHAT?'

'Lock us in the cellar? But we helped you make the cure.'

'Yes, and you caused all the trouble in the first place.'

'But to lock us up and leave us! You wouldn't do that!'

'Oh, yes I would!' Arthur grinned nastily. 'I'd enjoy it!'

The boys were astounded. This was a turn of events they had not expected. Was Arthur Venger a madman after all? They should never have accepted a lift from a stranger. Here they were, in a remote place where nobody would hear their cries for help. It was time to panic.

Then, as suddenly as it had changed before, Arthur Venger's mood changed again. He began to laugh merrily.

'It's all right. I was just trying out a few lies. I had to see if this stuff worked, and it does. We've done it!'

Herbie noticed the clock. 'But it's already half-past two. We're nearly too late.'

They made a hasty departure, leaving the house in a wild, untidy mess. They jumped into the car, and now Arthur, needing to drive, had to hand over the bottle of dark green liquid to Kip, who was sitting in the front seat.

'Just you be careful with that. A lot of people's futures depend on it, especially ours.'

They drove at a fast pace, back into town and out at the other side. Kip was sure they were speeding, and hoped they would not be spotted by their policeman.

The little red mini, followed by a yellow baker's van, had just turned into the lane that led up to school when the accident happened. There was a car coming fast down the middle of the lane towards them. Mr Venger pulled sharply over to the side to keep out of the way, then realized there was still not enough room. He pulled up in a screaming swerve, and the yellow van behind ran into the back of him.

The noise of the impact was much greater than the damage, but even so, Herbie was thrown forward from the back seat, so that his head butted Kip in the shoulder. Kip's arm jerked under his seat-belt, his door flew open and the green bottle shot from his grasp into the roadway, where it shattered and ran green into the gutter.

There was a stunned and terrible silence. Venger and the boys stared at the ruin of their plans.

Then the driver of the baker's van began shouting, and the tableau came to life. Arthur climbed out to inspect the damage and to exchange notes with the others. A little crowd of spectators began to gather.

Kip stared into the hedgerow, envious of the lucky dandelions, while Herbie tried to imagine what his mother would say when he told her he had been expelled from school.

The boys might have gone on sitting there, feeling sorry for themselves, if they had not heard the sound of an approaching police-car siren. In fresh panic, they scrambled from the car and started off at the double on the last half-mile to school.

8
The Purple-speckled Speech

The school orchestra had played its screeching best, the Chairman of the Governors had sat down, the last late parent had scurried to his seat, and Mr George Dykes, MA, had risen to address the Speech Day audience.

There was a respectful hush.

'I must say I am surprised,' Mr Dykes began, ignoring the sheaf of notes on the table beside him, 'to see so many of you here today. The pupils, of course, are here because they have no option, but as for you parents, I can't think why you bother. You must find the whole thing very boring.'

There were one or two shy giggles from the audience, who didn't quite know whether this was supposed to be a joke.

'However, now that you are here,' Mr Dykes went on, 'I suppose you will expect to hear me deliver my report upon the last school year. I'd much rather not. It wasn't a good year at all. In fact, I think the best word to describe it would be DISASTROUS. We didn't win a single cup. Our football first eleven lost all but two of its

games, our cricket team averaged seven runs a match, our girls' hockey eleven injured two referees and we couldn't even find a good enough competitor for the Inter-Schools' Chess Tournament.'

Some of the audience began to look interested. This was certainly an unusual approach to the year's achievements.

'At the last athletics meeting,' Mr Dykes went on, 'our runners came last in the hundred and two-hundred metres, our relay team was disqualified for cheating and our javelin thrower killed a sheep.

'On the academic side, perhaps we did a little better. We produced a language set which invented its own French dialect, and one star handwriting expert who managed to get his name in the Guinness Book of Records – on every page.'

By now a movement could be detected in the audience, a seething restlessness, as people turned to see what the general reaction was.

'You will be wondering what all this means,' continued Mr Dykes, warming to his subject. 'It means, quite simply, that this is not an exceptional school, alive with exceptional geniuses, but a draughty, shabby building where imperfect human beings make mistakes and fail examinations and let down their friends and feel ashamed, and wish they'd never heard of Saint Bede.'

'Hear, hear!' said a tiny voice at the back of the hall.

This produced a ripple of uneasy laughter and a creaking of chairs and a shuffling of feet. The reporter from the *Grumpton Argus* was seen to be scribbling furiously, and Mr Bigley, the Deputy Head, frowned fiercely round the hall to try to restore some sort of order.

Mr Dykes took a sip from his glass of water before proceeding.

'I could stand here telling you tales about boys and girls who have moved on from this school to Higher Education. Believe it or not, we do have a few. I usually spend half an hour boasting about their successes. But today I'm not going to. Today I'm going to give the true picture of everyday life in this school by describing instead a random sample of achievements.'

Mr Dykes glared around, as if daring anyone to stop him.

'In Form 4E, for instance, we have one boy who has broken no less than seventeen windows during his stay with us, yet still does not know the meaning of the word "fragile". In the same form, another boy has carved twenty-nine messages on our furniture, yet still cannot spell "united".'

By now the hall was holding its breath. There was a sense of alertness such as had never before been felt in a Speech Day gathering. Not one eye was closed, not one surreptitious comic was being read. Some people were actually beginning to enjoy themselves. Not Mr Bigley, though, and certainly not the Chairman of the Governors, who thought Mr Dykes had gone mad.

'We have one girl,' Mr Dykes was now saying, 'who has dyed her hair no less than five different colours in the space of one term. If that is not an achievement, I don't know what is.'

This time there were not even any giggles. Nobody wanted to make a sound, for that might cause them to miss the next sensation.

'In Form 3C we have a lad who has uprooted more young trees than any single vandal of his age in the whole of England, while in Form 3E the total number of days lost through truancy last year was nine hundred and four.'

That did it! Mr Bigley swung round in his seat and whispered to the woodwork master behind him, 'This has gone far enough! We must get him off the platform.'

'How?' the woodwork master whispered back.

'Take him a message, or something. Use your ingenuity, man!'

'Who, me?'

This was the moment at which Kip and Herbie tiptoed into the hall, having run all the way from the accident in the lane. They had not tiptoed far before they saw their worst fears were realized. Mr Dykes really had started telling the truth.

'Each year I talk about the parents' role in education,' he was saying now. 'A most important role. This year I'd like to begin at the beginning with the naming of the child. One boy in this school has been given, for instance, an author's surname for his own first name. Now, I want you to think . . .'

Inspired by the sheer horror of the situation, Kip shot forward and grabbed Mr Bigley by the arm.

'Sir!' shouted Kip. 'There's a dangerous explosive device in the hall. I think you ought to clear the building.'

64

9
An Explosive Afternoon

Normally, Mr Bigley would have quelled such a disturbance with one cold and terrifying look. Today, however, he felt only that his prayers had been answered.

At once he leapt on to the platform and requested an orderly evacuation of the building. The explosive device would probably turn out to be harmless, he said, but of course they could take no chances. The Speech Day ceremony was postponed until further notice.

People began at once to scramble to their feet. Teachers barked orders and classes started to file out of the hall at a much brisker pace than usual. Most parents looked flustered, but they soon got the hang of things and began following their offspring to the exits. It was a wonderful display of discipline and self-control, a well-rehearsed performance which the *Grumpton Argus* would be obliged to admire.

Mr Bigley then had time to turn his attention to the Headmaster. Where was he? And how quickly could he be spirited away before he said anything more? Mr Dykes had led his platform party in a brisk but dignified withdrawal to the far side of the front lawn, and was there discovered guarding the school's new mini-computer which had only just been paid for.

'Are you all right, Headmaster?'

'Of course I'm all right, Bigley. What the dickens is going on?'

'Everything is under control,' answered Mr Bigley evasively, 'but I think you had better come along to the sports pavilion where you'll be safe. I'll round up the other VIPs to join you there. Perhaps Mrs Emmett could lay on some tea.'

'Tea?' echoed the irate Headmaster. 'It's police we need, not tea. Let me know the minute they arrive. I'll talk to them.'

'But, Headmaster, I think you should . . .'

'Don't stand there chattering, Bigley! This is an emergency!'

It was obvious that poor Mr Bigley's efforts to spirit the Head away were useless. He could only hope that in the confusion nobody would remember what Mr Dykes had said, or take notice of anything else he might say from now on.

Meantime, reporters from the *Grumpton Argus* and the *County News* were bombarding Cedric Clodd with questions. Did Cedric feel that the present emergency had been aimed at him? Was this bomb a wicked attempt by his political opponents to prevent him from making his speech?

Cedric would have loved to say yes. He longed to feel important enough for an assassination attempt. Unfortunately, he had arrived late owing to a rail strike, had had no time for lunch, and had therefore been given a quick cup of tea and a slice of Truthpaste cake just before he went on to the platform. When he opened his mouth to agree with the reporters, he suddenly found that he could not. All that emerged from his throat was a croak like cracking ice. Most embarrassing!

Luckily for Cedric, the reporters' attention was diverted by a bandaged Arthur Venger, who now rushed upon the scene, crying loudly:

'It's all my fault!'

Naturally, the reporters thought Arthur was about to confess to planting the bomb, and they turned eagerly towards him, pencils poised.

'Truthpaste, that's the trouble!' cried Arthur, seeing chaos and fearing the worst. He plunged feverishly into his story, wanting only to make a clean breast of the whole thing.

It was an amazing story. It was the sort of story that newspaper reporters dream about, whilst they are writing up vicarage garden fêtes and local weddings and amateur operatic performances. It was, in fact, a scoop, which could have made not only the local headlines, but the national and international ones as well. The only snag was that the two reporters did not believe it. Faced with the pure, unvarnished truth, they could do no more than throw long-suffering glances at one another behind Arthur Venger's back, and quietly conclude that the man was crackers.

Meanwhile, someone had dialled 999, and soon the screech of sirens heralded the arrival of police and ambulance. Kip and Herbie, waylaid by Mr Bigley, were dragged forth to tell their story – to the very same policeman who had haunted them all day.

The policeman groaned. 'I don't believe it!'

'Anything wrong, Constable?'

'It's these kids, Sarge. Known offenders. Ten to one you'll find they're at the bottom of everything.'

'All right, leave 'em to me. You go and locate the explosive device and get the details down.'

The sergeant turned to Kip and Herbie with a suspiciously friendly smile.

'Now then, lads, let's hear from you. WHAT explosive device are we talking about exactly?'

Kip looked hunted. He licked his lips carefully before replying: 'It was Mr Dykes, sir. He could have brought the house down at any minute. We felt he was a human explosive device.'

10
The Final Truth

That evening, St Bede's Church Hall was packed for Cedric Clodd's address. Word had gone round of the afternoon's excitement, and people thought Cedric really had been the cause of the trouble. So everyone was here to see what further thrills might happen.

As for Cedric himself, he had been deprived of his afternoon glory and was determined to make up for it tonight. This would be the best speech he had ever made. His words would ring with high ideals and loyalty and self-sacrifice, and at the end he would be given a standing ovation.

'Ladies and gentlemen, constituents, friends,' he began. 'The true purpose of my being here tonight . . .'

There followed a sort of croaking sound, then a long, alarming pause. Had Cedric, perhaps, been poisoned? There was a stir of interest. Then the words that Cedric had planned to say mysteriously changed themselves into very different words.

'The true purpose of my being here tonight is to show off. I love showing off. Best of all, I enjoy the sound of my own voice. (You must admit I have perfect elocution and my words carry clearly to the farthest corners of the hall.) I don't really care about your problems, although now and again I pretend to, so that you won't forget to vote for me next time. I also need to do a bit of work for you now and then in order to get my name into the newspapers. (That's something I *do* enjoy, as long as they spell it properly.) But really, you know, this is a very boring job, especially the journeys I have to make up here. What a dump this town is! I can't think how you can stand living here!'

There were shouts of shock and protest from the audience.

'How dare he talk to us like that?'

'Well, at least he's honest,' one voter yelled above the rest. 'That's more than you can say for most.'

'Oh yes, I'm honest all right!' retorted Cedric, surprising even himself. 'I'm so honest that I'll tell you all, here and now, that I'm no good to you. I possess none of the qualities of a useful Member of Parliament. In fact, now I come to think of it, the best advice I can give you is not to vote for me at the next election after all. Not even if I'm the only candidate.'

'Can't say fairer than that!' cried somebody in the front row.

'No, by Jove, I've never heard such straight talk from a politician.'

'Here's a chap we can actually believe at last.'

'True as steel, he is!'

'Genuine as Harris tweed!'

'He's another George Washington, bless his spotless soul!'

There was no doubt that the crowd was impressed. The comments grew warmer and more generous, until somebody burst into song. In no time at all the crowd was singing with gusto:

'For he's a jolly good fellow

And so say all of us!'

At the back of the hall, Kip, Herbie and Arthur Venger looked astoundedly at one another. Arthur began to steer the boys towards the door.

'Come on, this is no place for us! May as well go and get on with that litter-dropping cure. See if that will be less of a disaster than the Truthpaste has turned out to be.'

'Oh, I don't know,' replied Herbie the genius thoughtfully. 'It may not be such a disaster as you think. Suppose we sold it to the Russians . . .?'

But that's another story.

The
Choking Peril

By Hazel Townson
ILLUSTRATED BY DAVID McKEE

Contents

For the Codd super-family of Newark
Pauline, Mike, Debbie, Stewart, Emma and Nicky

1
Seeds of an Idea

'There's far too much litter about,' grumbled Arthur Venger. 'Just look at my garden, filled with bus tickets and lolly sticks and toffee papers. As for the pavement outside my gate, it looks like the end of a market day.' He began stuffing into a huge plastic bag the disgusting objects which lay strewn around. One screwed-up newspaper, smelling of chips; one rotting carrot; two squashed coke tins; three cigarette packets; four apple cores . . . .

Just as he reached out for a particularly nasty-looking hunk of mouldy bread, young Kip Slater said, 'I thought you were working on a cure for litter-dropping?'

Kip and his friend, Herbie Coswell, had come to call on Arthur in the hope of being able to help with one of his experiments. For Arthur Venger was a unique combination of chemist, inventor, salesman and crusader, bent on trying to improve the world. With this improvement in mind, he usually had some sort of experiment on the go. The boys had become involved with one of these experiments at their last school Speech Day, and were now Arthur's devoted admirers.

'I *have* worked on lots of cures for litter-dropping,

that's true,' admitted Arthur. 'From the simple Tidy Bag, which everyone could carry round like they used to carry gas-masks during the last war (you'll have noticed *I've* always got a Tidy Bag) to a very much more complicated scientific experiment. But as my last Truthpaste experiment was such a disaster, I haven't had the heart to try this new one out.'

'Well, I think you should,' pronounced Herbie Coswell the genius. 'It's like falling off a horse. You should get back on again straight away, before you lose your nerve. What you need is somebody to give you back your confidence. We can do that.'

'I'll say we can!' agreed Kip enthusiastically. 'I don't honestly think Tidy Bags would catch on. People wouldn't be bothered. But a real scientific experiment is a different matter. Let's try it! We've got terrific faith in you, and six weeks' holiday to spare.'

Arthur looked unconvinced, but at that moment a car drew up alongside his bit of pavement, the driver opened the door, tipped out the contents of his ashtray on to the space that Arthur had just cleared, then drove away again. Arthur flung down his bag in disgusted amazement.

'Right! That does it!'

Inviting the boys to follow him, he marched into the kitchen of his bungalow and opened the EXPERI-MENTAL ONLY cupboard. From this cupboard Arthur took out a huge glass jar filled with tiny brown seeds. 'These,' he explained importantly, 'are the seeds of my very own, incredible, fast-growing weed which I've christened Litterwort. That Litterwort will spring up fast and furious wherever it happens to fall. It creeps. Well, no; it doesn't so much creep as *gallop*! It will roam over concrete and marble and plastic and glass. In fact, there's only one place it won't grow, and that is where I've sprayed my other equally staggering product, ALIWOS.' Here, Arthur produced an object like an orange-coloured hairspray can and waved it in the air.

'Anti-Litterwort-Spray, of course,' Herbie the genius translated before Kip had even begun to wonder what ALIWOS meant.

'Now,' continued Arthur, 'what we have to do is *punish* the litter-droppers. If they can't see that litter makes a mess of their town, perhaps they'll see that Litterwort *does*. If we could manage to put these seeds into likely bits of litter, then spray the insides of *litter bins only* with ALIWOS, I think we would soon be able to teach the public better manners. With thick weeds growing everywhere and choking everything up, they'd have to stop and think. Especially since we'd also put up posters everywhere, saying: LITTER BREEDS LITTERWORT. YOU STOP THROWING—THE WEEDS STOP GROWING.'

'NO WEEDS GROW IN—A LITTER BIN,' added Kip, who had not been christened Kipling for nothing.

'H'm! Not a bad idea!' pronounced Herbie thoughtfully. 'There'd always be enough busybodies to take up the challenge and bully everyone else into being tidy. Your main problem, of course, would be getting your seeds into the public's hands. You'd better leave that to us. We'll distribute them for you.'

Kip looked sceptical. 'Do you mean to say we'd have to put one of these seeds inside every cigarette packet, every toffee paper, every lump of orange peel . . .?'

Herbie sighed. 'Use your brains. How could we? What we would have to do is fix our own special items of litter. Give out something which people are likely to throw away. We could have a flag day, for instance. Every flag folded double with a seed inside it.'

'That wouldn't work,' retorted Kip. 'Most of the people I know who buy flags—(and that's not many these days)—hang on to them like Superglue so they won't have to buy another. My Uncle Colin even saves his Remembrance Day poppy and irons the petals for next year.'

'Then he's tighter than a thumb-screw and doesn't deserve to live in a free country,' Herbie sneered. 'But I suppose you're right—flags are not really litter.' He pondered further until inspiration struck again. 'All right then, free gifts! With seeds in the wrappers. When folks open the gifts and throw down the wrappers they throw down the seeds as well.'

'Free gifts? That's going to cost us a fortune.'

12

'It needn't. I've got a drawer at home stuffed full of free gifts from cornflake packets, soap powder offers, etc. So have you, Kip. Then there's the stuff we got for presents and didn't want. Toys we've grown out of.'

'People are going to be mighty suspicious if we just start giving things away,' warned Arthur. 'They'll think there's a catch in it and refuse to take one. I knew a man who stood on a street corner once for a bet, offering real fivers for sale at 50p each, and nobody would buy one. They didn't want to look foolish.'

'But suppose we had a good reason for giving things away?'

Herbie's face suddenly glowed. 'Grumpton Carnival!' he cried, referring to an annual event that was due in a few weeks' time. 'You could dress up as Father Christmas, Mr Venger, and give out presents then. People would think it was all part of the Carnival fun. Kip and I could be your helpers. Reindeer or something.'

'I'm not being the back half of a reindeer.'

'All right, snowmen then.'

'H'm!' mused Arthur. 'It might just work. The Carnival procession starts and finishes in the park, and Bert Higgs, the Park Superintendent, told me he'd had to move fifteen tons of litter after last year's Carnival. If we gave out the presents there, it would be a good start to our plan. The Litterwort would soon take hold in the park. And we could stick our posters on all the gates, seats, fences and shelters.' He rubbed his hands with growing excitement. 'I'll buy some real gifts, too. May as well do the thing properly. I'll get my money back in the end, because people will have to pay me to spray my ALIWOS, and I intend that to be mighty expensive.'

Arthur began a list of all the things they would need. 'One—presents. You bring what you can—(good quality stuff, mind; nothing damaged or dirty)—then leave the rest to me. Two—wrapping paper; sheets and sheets of it.'

'I'll take care of that,' Kip volunteered. 'My mum saves all the paper off our Christmas and birthday presents ready to use again. She has a suitcase full.'

'What a family!' sneered Herbie. 'Does she iron that as well?'

'Waste not, want not!' Kip retorted loyally.

'Three—a Father Christmas outfit,' continued Arthur. 'That can be hired. Maybe the snowmen's costumes can, too. If not, we could easily make something out of papier-mâché and cotton wool. As for the posters, we'll work on those together.'

'We're in business!' cried Herbie. The triumphant gleam in his eye was a beacon to banish holiday boredom.

'Pity about the park, though. I rather like it,' mused Kip. 'I can't fancy the swings and boating pool and rose garden all thick with horrible weeds. Not to

14

mention the bandstand and the bit where we play cricket.'

'Well, don't forget we can soon put things to rights when people have learned their lesson,' Arthur Venger reassured him. 'A huge dose of ALIWOS and all will be well. See what it says on the ALIWOS spray? "It kills as it spills." Litterwort only, of course.'

'It slays as it sprays,' improved Herbie.

'It slaughters as it waters,' capped Kip. 'Bags I the ALIWOS spray to squirt round the litter bins.' But Arthur said he had better do that bit himself, as mistakes at this stage would be fatal.

A slow grin spread itself across Arthur Venger's face, and his bright blue eyes began to twinkle. 'I'm going to enjoy every minute of this!' Little did he know how wrong he was.

2
A Budding Crime

'The best day for a robbery,' said Mungo Slye, 'is Carnival Day.' He tapped with the tip of his pencil at the spot on his map where Grumpton Museum was marked. Mungo had already ringed this spot in red.

Perce O'Deary looked worried. 'But Mungo,' he complained, 'the museum's right opposite the park. That's where the Carnival procession starts and finishes, and after that there's the fair and the band and the fireworks and I-don't-know-what, all in the park. Everybody will be there.'

'Exactly!' Mungo smirked. 'Plenty of riot, noise and hullabaloo! Just what we need to cover up our little bit of business. Furthermore, all the police will be otherwise engaged, keeping the Carnival crowds in order.'

'But the Carnival's on Bank Holiday Monday. The museum will be closed.'

Mungo cast his eyes towards the ceiling and said in long-suffering tones, 'I suppose you expected us to walk into a museum full of people and make our snatch with everybody watching?' Really, Mungo sometimes wondered why he didn't take hold of Perce O'Deary and shake him until his dandruff went into orbit. Mungo had to remind himself that he needed an

assistant who was not bright enough to realise what was going on, especially the value of the loot involved. Mungo must try to be nice to Perce until the whole daring plot was safely carried out.

'Carnivals mean dressing up. Fancy costumes,' explained Mungo patiently. 'That suits us fine. We'll dress up as burglars, with check caps and black eye-masks and sacks stuffed with newspaper, saying SWAG in big, red letters. Then we'll mingle all afternoon, so that everybody sees us. When they see us again at night with the real swag, they'll take no notice.'

'Mingle?' Perce echoed doubtfully. He didn't know what mingle meant, but guessed it had something to do with the Carnival Morris dancing. Mungo had asked Perce if he was light-fingered. Should he have said light-footed?

'We'll mix with the crowd,' said Mungo slowly, as if to a child of three. 'We'll walk about the park and enjoy ourselves, like everybody else. Then when it's dark and the fireworks start, we'll slip round to the back of the museum. I'll deal with the burglar alarm while you keep watch, just like we practised yesterday. Then I'll cut out a window-pane and Bob's your uncle. I'll be in and out again in fifteen minutes with the Baron in my sack.'

Perce peered through a fog of bewilderment. At last he muttered: 'But Mungo, my uncle's called George.'

Mungo ground his teeth, yet forced himself to grin,

giving Perce's shoulder a soothing pat.

Of course, Mungo did not intend to stuff a real, live Baron into his sack; only the Baron's wax bust which had been set up in the museum by a grateful Town Council. For Baron Banks was Grumpton's most illustrious inhabitant. Not only had he become world famous for his invention of the micro-celery-silencer, thereby turning himself almost overnight into a millionaire, but he had then bestowed his riches liberally on the town, providing a swimming pool, a museum and two new football pitches, as well as fountains, flagpoles and floral displays galore. The bust, proudly placed in the entrance-hall of the new museum, was the expression of the townsfolk's gratitude.

Some people might think that a wax bust was a strange thing to steal. Yet there was method in Mungo's madness. Mungo worked as a clerk in a solicitor's office, and had been given the job of filing away Baron Banks's will. Being a naturally inquisitive person, Mungo soon discovered two sensational facts. Firstly, that Baron Banks had secretly bought the magnificent Eyeball Diamond, one of the rarest jewels in the world, so-called because it resembled a human eyeball in shape and size. Secondly, that the Baron, who was fond of practical jokes and had no family of his own, had bequeathed this diamond to 'the Grumptonian who manages to find it first', thus promising to set in motion a splendid treasure hunt after his death. Naturally, so far nobody knew about all this except the Baron, his solicitor and Mungo. The solicitor was as good at keeping secrets as a doctor or a priest. He would already have shut out of his mind all details of the Baron's will, which gave Mungo a head start in the treasure hunt. The will did not say *when* the diamond should be found. So why wait until Baron Banks's death, by which time there would be thousands searching for it? The moment to find it was *now*.

Being a well-trained villain, Mungo kept his eyes and ears open at all times, ever ready to profit from the folly, greed and carelessness of other people. For instance, he had spent a great deal of time in Grumpton museum, trying to decide which objects were worth stealing. Whilst there, he had gradually come to notice that when the sun was in a certain position, so that its rays fell through the stained-glass window on to the Baron's bust, the eye behind the monocle winked and sparkled in a strange and lively way. Far too strange or lively for glass or plastic. Could this be the vital clue?

It was well known that the eccentric Baron often visited his bust, whispering in its ear and patting it on the head. He could so easily, on some quiet Monday morning, have gouged out the plastic eyeball from behind the plastic monocle and substituted the Eyeball Diamond, suitably painted over with a dark brown eye.

At any rate, that was Mungo's guess. Now he could

prove himself right. What a coup it would be to steal the Eyeball Diamond! What a feat of intelligence and daring! And what a smart way to ensure that Mungo could live happily ever after without doing another stroke of work! No more nine-to-five sessions in a dusty office. No more putting up with thick-headed messenger-boys like Perce O'Deary, who always got everything wrong and left Mungo to take the blame. Nothing but peace, leisure and luxury for ever!

Mungo knew that if he was to break into the museum, he needed a look-out ... somebody who would not guess what he was really up to. The perfect candidate was Perce O'Deary, the world's most muddled non-thinker, who could easily be persuaded that Mungo was 'borrowing' the bust as part of a charity rag, to raise money for the local Children's Home. The museum would have to buy back the bust by giving money to the Home, he told Perce.

'Nothing in it for us, of course. We're just helping the kiddies.'

Perce, who had been brought up at the Children's Home, thought this was a great idea.

Mungo's first plan had been to prise out the precious diamond from its socket. On second thoughts, he decided he might scratch and damage it. Anyway, prising it out might take too long. Better to steal the whole bust instead. Baron Banks's bust would just fit nicely into the sack marked SWAG. And since the

Baron was at present away on a world cruis
would realise the significance of the theft until M
had got clean away.

3
oming Fireworks

mpton Carnival dawned bright and
wind, ... e right weather for scattering seeds.
Crowds converged upon the town from miles around.
Full car parks, traffic jams and pavements packed with
procession-watchers turned the town into a simmering
pot of trouble. Pick-pockets, handbag-snatchers and
vendors of reject balloons wove in and out upon their
villainous errands. Toni's Ices doubled their prices.
Harpo's Hot Dogs shrank to half their usual size. Yet
none of this seemed to dampen the festive spirit. People
were determined to enjoy themselves and to forget
their everyday cares. For weeks, all had looked forward
to this event, and they jolly well intended to make the
most of it, especially the free presents from Father
Christmas and his snowmen. Something for nothing!
That was the way to set the fingers grabbing!

'Pink for girls, blue for boys, purple for grown-ups.
Only one each *please,* madam! I don't care if you *have*
got forty-nine grandchildren. And please put your
litter in the bins, or you'll start a plague of weeds.'

It took less than an hour for Arthur and his helpers
to dispose of a bulging sackful of presents, and dozens of
screwed-up wrappers were already bowling merrily

24

over the flower-beds and out through the railings.

'Well, we've done it now! By tomorrow morning this town won't know what's hit it!'

Arthur went back to his car for a second sack-load, pushing his way through a colourful mixture of Red Indians, pirates, fairies and Romans. He even met a human giraffe, a walking toadstool and a couple of burglars. Arthur had to chuckle at the sacks marked SWAG. One good thing about the annual Carnival was that it brought out people's ingenuity as well as their litter. 'In fact, this year,' chuckled Arthur to himself, 'they'll get more ingenuity than they ever bargained for.'

The fireworks began at nine o'clock in the evening, when the sky was dark enough to show them at their best. Grumpton Carnival was famed for its wonderful firework display, and heads turned upwards from miles around to watch the winking, soaring, crackling patterns of colour.

Mungo Slye's head was no exception. He, too, was watching the fireworks from a spot near the park's main gates, but he was not watching for pleasure. Mungo was waiting for the bigger bangs to start, so that he could set about his thieving. A noise to hide a noise, as Mungo's mother used to say when young Mungo turned up the radio volume to cover the crunch of his shop-lifted toffees.

Stars burst and rockets fizzed and flew. Pink and

blue balls cascaded on to tree-tops and away on the skyline Mungo could see the Carnival bonfire glowing orange and red at the other end of the park.

At last there came a great explosion, followed by an upward thrust of sparks. Then crack-crack-crack, and bang, and boom, and crack-crack-crack again. Now was the moment! Mungo grabbed Perce's arm and hurried him away through the upward-gazing crowd, out of the park gates, across the road and round to the back of the museum. The cobbled back street was deserted. The museum sat dark and silent in the middle of a row of closed-up banks and shops and offices. Setting down his sack, Mungo shook out all the screwed-up newspapers he had filled it with, then folded the sack, stuffed it inside his jacket, and began work very gently on the burglar alarm.

Perce, his head still reeling with the fireworks, took up his post at the end of the back street, supposedly keeping watch. But every time another rocket shot into the air, so did Perce's gaze. A blind old woman could have picked Perce's pocket and he wouldn't have noticed.

At last, Mungo had the window out. He set the pane down gently on the pavement, then climbed in through the gap, groping his way carefully until he felt it was safe to switch on his torch.

It seemed a long way round to the entrance hall at the front of the building. For a while, Mungo thought

27

he must have taken a wrong turning, but he came out at last in the high-windowed hall where the bust of Baron Banks had pride of place. A sudden firework flash lit up the room, and Mungo saw clearly the Baron's waxen head with its thick, white hair, its moustache, its monocle—and behind the monocle its fiercely sparkling eye. It was an eerie sight. There was Mungo, alone in that silent room, with an eye that seemed to be watching every move he made. A good thing Mungo was not a fanciful man! He found it much more natural to think of all the things he would be able to buy with that Eyeball once he had sold it. Top quality hand-sewn suits; regular subscriptions to all the comic papers; a set of fishing tackle; a bungalow with gnomes and a goldfish pond; a blue-and-green-striped sports car . . . .

Now he had actually reached the pedestal on which the bust stood. Now he had his hands round the Baron's slippery, waxen throat. Whoops! He almost dropped it! But at last he had the Baron safely in his sack, and was making his getaway.

When Mungo reached the empty back window-frame, he checked that Perce O'Deary was still standing at the end of the road, exactly where Mungo had left him. Yes! Good lad! He was still there . . . but wait a minute! What was Perce O'Deary doing? He was actually standing there chatting to a policeman! The policeman had interrupted his beat to spend a com-

panionable moment swapping comments with Perce about the novelty of Perce's costume and the quality of this year's fireworks. The two of them were getting on like a colony of ants.

Mungo stepped back in alarm. For a while he hid and waited, his poor heart banging as hard as a coffin-maker's hammer in a plague.

The policeman showed no signs of moving on. In fact, he had taken quite a fancy to Perce, who was wondering whether to tell him about the charity rag. Mungo decided he would have to let himself out by the front door and run off in the other direction. He had seen a bunch of keys hanging up in the Curator's office. Snatching these up, he tried every single one in the front door lock, without success. That meant he would have to remove another pane of glass and climb out by one of the front windows. 'Let's hope nobody's watching!' thought Mungo. 'Not that I've any choice.' Mungo had just removed this second pane of glass, thrown his laden sack through on to the pavement outside, and put one leg over the sill ready to follow the sack, when Perce's friendly policeman appeared in the hall.

'Now then, what's all this?'

Mungo was caught, and it wasn't even a fair cop. It was all Perce O'Deary's fault. One day Mungo would throttle Perce—but not for a while yet, by the looks of things.

4
A Bunch of Trouble

Arthur Venger set his alarm clock for the very crack of dawn. By then the Litterwort should have grown quite well, and Arthur wanted to be the first to see the results. Kip Slater and Herbie Coswell had also arranged to wake up early, so that Arthur could pick them up in his car on the way to the park. After all, the lads had helped with the presents, and with the pasting-up of posters after dark, so they deserved to be in on the fun.

Arthur yawned and stretched, touching his toes three times rather creakily before parting the curtains. At first all seemed right with the world, but when he rubbed his eyes and looked again, he saw that even here, such a long distance from the park, weeds were already springing up in the cracks between the pavings and starting their forward crawl. One particularly savage clump had climbed half-way up a wall and had already obscured the LITTER BREEDS LITTER-WORT sign. A better result than Arthur had hoped for! Chuckling delightedly, he dressed, gulped down his cornflakes and coffee, then hurried to his car. This would teach everyone a lesson, and no mistake.

Arthur lived on the outskirts of Grumpton, but as he drove nearer to the centre of the town he found the

going more and more difficult, for patches of ever-thicker and more tangled weeds loomed in his path. In some places it was like trying to drive through a blackberry bush. By the time he reached the road where Kip and Herbie lived, he was having a very bumpy ride and decided to leave his car and walk. Of course, Arthur had brought with him a can of ALI-WOS and could have cleared a patch for himself if he had wanted to. But that would have made things easier for everyone else as well, and you don't teach people a lesson by making things easier for them, Arthur reasoned. So Arthur stepped out of his car.

At once, a strange thing happened. Arthur took a deep breath—and stood entranced! What was that wonderful smell? He breathed again. The smell seemed even more wonderful. Not a smell, but a perfume, a rich, sweet, magical scent that made him feel totally happy. For quite a few moments he could do nothing but stand and draw in deep lungfuls of the heady stuff, smiling with closed eyes at the wonder of it all.

A perfumed weed! The Litterwort was perfumed! This was something Arthur had never even thought of. In the experimental stages, he had grown only one or two shoots of the stuff, and as he had had a cold at the time he had never noticed any perfume. But this! Why, it was a miracle! If it made everyone feel as happy as he felt at this moment, then it must be worth a fortune. It was even prettily coloured; most pleasant to look upon.

Six petals on each opening flower were ranged in alternate pinks and yellows and blues. Greedily, Arthur plucked a bunch of Litterwort and held it to his nose. He strewed it on his car seat, stuck it in his buttonhole, his belt, his pockets. He was almost delirious with joy.

This was how Kip and Herbie found him, having spotted Arthur from the top of Kip's garden wall, which they had had to climb because the gateway was choked with weeds. The boys were already over-excited.

'Some weed, Mr Venger!'

'Why didn't you tell us it would be like this?'

'I didn't know!' breathed Arthur, shaking his head incredulously. His brain buzzed wildly with the new possibilities. Here was not merely something to clog up the roads and create a nuisance. Here was a positive contribution to the quality of life, as valuable as fine food and drink, good holidays, great music, paintings, poetry. Not what Arthur had intended at all.

Herbie had seen a few possibilities, too. 'This stuff must be worth a fortune! A pity you didn't just grow yourself a gardenful, Mr Venger, so you could have sold it. Now it belongs to everybody. It's theirs for the picking.'

'We could go round with the ALIWOS spray,' suggested Kip, 'and kill it all off. Then start again, just planting seeds in Mr Venger's garden.'

Arthur shook his head, dispelling the daydreams.

'That wouldn't do much to solve the litter problem, would it? And anyway, it would take far too long. The world would be astir long before we'd finished.' Indeed, it was already too late, for as he spoke a nearby door opened and a sleepy Fred Jepps, the local milkman, began to amble slowly up a weed-strewn path on his way to the dairy.

Fred was more than usually tired this morning, having stayed late at the Carnival the night before. In fact, he felt quite stupefied with weariness, and stopped in mid-pathway to rub his eyes and yawn. Then all of a sudden Fred Jepps woke up. He sniffed. He turned his head and sniffed again. He took a deep breath, like a diver about to plunge from the top board. At last he swung round and headed back to the house, calling excitedly to his wife: 'Hey, Millie, something's happened to our garden!'

'There you are!' commented Arthur sadly. 'Ten more minutes and the whole town will know.'

'Ten minutes!' groaned Herbie. 'That's all it takes to lose a fortune!'

Mungo Slye had also lost a fortune. He had been whisked off to the police station hours ago, without a chance to recover the bust in the sack. As far as he knew, it still lay there, on the pavement, waiting for the first passer-by to pick it up. Perce O'Deary's policeman

friend, P.C. Dribble, had caught Mungo with one leg over the museum window-sill and borne him triumphantly off for questioning without even looking through the window. Mungo was the first criminal he had ever caught, and P.C. Dribble could not wait to show him off to his Inspector. None of them could have guessed that the sack was already well-hidden under a thickening crop of Litterwort.

Next door to the milkman lived Eddie Sellars, a travelling market trader. Eddie was due that morning at the market in the neighbouring town of Lyckham. Eddie sold second-hand books; dog-eared paperbacks, musty old tomes with their backs hanging off, and so on. But today, hearing the racket made by his neighbour and quickly taking in what had happened, he decided to switch products. He would sell Litterwort instead. Eddie kept this idea to himself, but great minds began to think alike. Other Grumpton stallholders awoke, and began loading up their vans, not with rolls of cloth or antiques or vegetables as usual, but with great bunches of Litterwort, plus buckets, tins, vases and basins to keep them in. This Litterwort was suddenly a far more valuable product than anything they had ever sold before. Nor did it seem to matter that every Grumpton stallholder had had the same idea. For, once they all arrived at the market in Lyckham, it soon became clear that the Litterwort would go faster than free fritters in a famine. The cost rose from 50p a bunch to 50p a sprig. Then £1 a sprig, then £2, £5, £10—what a ridiculous way to make a fortune!

The news—and of course the wonderful smell—spread far and wide, and Lyckham market place was soon jammed with people. Some drove in from as far as a hundred miles away, having been telephoned by friends. Some moved like zombies in a trance, sniffing with closed eyes and great smiles of bliss. Fantastic sums of money were offered for the fragrant weeds, and the minute any stallholder sold out all he had to do was to rush back to Grumpton and pick another batch.

Arthur Venger, who had seen what was happening and followed the crowd, was now seized by a new worry. The whole thing was getting out of hand. He had not foreseen that people would actually *want* the Litterwort and carry it off to places where he would never be able to reach it.

'We must stop them buying it!' he cried distractedly to the boys.

So Herbie and Kip, misunderstanding, went around whispering in people's ears, telling them that they had no need to buy the stuff; they could just drive another couple of miles up the road and they would be able to pick it for themselves.

There was instant pandemonium. Cars drove off by the dozen, honking and swerving in the race to be there

38

first. Soon the road into Grumpton became hopelessly jammed. Vehicles were abandoned where they stood, and drivers ran the rest of the way, leaping ecstatically at last into knee-deep verges of Litterwort. There, seized with a greedy madness, everyone began plucking and wrenching and sawing with penknives at the tough young stems. The mass of busy, bending bodies eventually pushed its way right into the centre of the town.

Now came the chaos which Arthur had intended, yet it came not from surging weeds, but from surging weeders. Every street was blocked with people. Innocent townsfolk could not even open their own front doors to nip and grab a bit of Litterwort for themselves. It was outrageous! Something would have to be done!

The telephone wires hummed with frantic messages, and at last, with enormous difficulty, the Mayor and a few of the councillors managed to make their way to the Town Hall for an emergency meeting. They all agreed that they couldn't put up with this state of affairs, but what was the solution?

'We'll have to push back these crowds and close off the town!'

'Nonsense! This is wonderful for trade!' retorted a councillor who happened to own a couple of supermarkets. 'All these pickers are getting hot and tired and thirsty. They'll need drinks and snacks and ice-creams and lunches and carrier-bags and bundles of string and sticking-plasters and picture postcards and I-don't-know-what. We've never done such good business for years.'

'It's no use making a fortune if you don't live to enjoy it,' observed the Mayor. 'Half the Grumptonians are going to be trampled to death at this rate. And what if a fight breaks out? It only needs A to lurch into B, and B to push him off, and you've got a riot on your hands.'

'Well, the answer is simple enough. If we get rid of these weeds the crowds will go. Can't we put some lawnmowers on to the roads? Or bulldozers or something?'

'Here, not so fast! Have you lost your sense of smell, or what? This stuff is the best thing that has ever happened to us. If we use our brains now we can make a fortune . . . .'

'Those who have *got* any brains can surely see . . . .'

At this moment the door of the Mayor's parlour burst open and a hot, dishevelled Arthur Venger appeared, waving a bag of seeds in one hand and an ALIWOS spray in the other. Arthur was a man with a conscience. When he felt he had done wrong he was anxious to confess and take his punishment. Kip and Herbie knew this, but felt that such impulsiveness would only lead to further trouble. They both came panting in behind Arthur, trying their best to restrain him.

'It's all my fault! I'm the one to blame!' Arthur shouted guiltily, and before the boys could stop him he had poured out the whole tragic tale.

'It's not really his fault,' objected Herbie. 'You can't stop weeds from growing if they want to.'

'It's everybody else's fault, for not putting their litter in the bins,' agreed Kip. 'You've seen what it says on the posters.'

'What posters?' asked a man who never read such things, on principle.

'Thought they were just a Carnival joke,' said someone else. 'Or the work of cranks and nutters. Plenty of those about these days.'

The Mayor, desperately trying to make sense of all this, began to remember a certain Speech Day at St. Bede's school, which he had attended some weeks ago. There had been some very funny goings-on at that Speech Day, and surely this was the man who had claimed responsibility? In which case, nothing was impossible, especially if these were also the same two lads who had been mixed up in the trouble. The Mayor pushed forward a plant-pot containing a wilting geranium. Plucking the geranium from the soil, he offered the pot to Arthur. 'Fast-growing seeds, you say? Go on then, give us a bit of proof. Let's see for ourselves.'

Arthur dropped a handful of seeds into the pot and pressed them down with his fingers. The Mayor watered them with a little can which he kept on top of his

filing cabinet. Then everyone stared hard at the pot.

'I don't see anything growing.'

'He's having you on!'

Arthur began to sweat. These people seemed determined to make him look foolish. If only they understood!

'We can't stand about all day, waiting for seeds to grow. We've got a crisis on our hands.'

Distractedly, Arthur mopped his brow, and Herbie Coswell, feeling sorry for him, stepped into the breach, crying: 'Give it time! No seed grows that fast. Even Jack's beanstalk took all night. Why don't you have a coffee-break, or something?'

So that was what the party did, mooching off to the Town Hall canteen with sceptical faces. Yet half an hour later, when they all trooped back again, sure enough there was the tip of a tiny shoot showing above the soil in the pot. The Mayor bent over it. He sniffed. Then a great smile spread across his face, multiplying his chins from two to four.

'Let that be a lesson to all of you! Always give the benefit of the doubt. Without my restraining influence you'd all have gone rushing off, and we'd never have known we were sitting on a gold mine.' He turned to the wretched Arthur and slapped him heartily on the back. 'My boy, I'm proud to know you! You're a greater asset to this town than Baron Banks himself.'

'But don't you understand...?' began Arthur

44

desperately, only to be shouted down by the Mayor's firm reasoning: 'What's to stop you spraying a ring of that ALIWOS stuff round Grumpton? Then we'd be sure the Litterwort would grow nowhere else but here. We could cultivate it properly and charge outsiders to come and smell it. In nice, orderly queues, of course.'

'We could use the ALIWOS to clear the roads, and just let the stuff go on growing in the park,' cried someone else.

'I think you're forgetting something,' said Herbie Coswell the genius at the top of his voice. 'That Litterwort has already been sold at Lyckham market, to all sorts of people living outside the town. It's been carried off in cars for miles and miles. The seeds will scatter everywhere. The whole country—nay, probably the whole world—will soon be covered in the stuff. We are quite possibly witnessing the end of civilisation as we know it!'

'Cor!' said Kip.

5
A Flowery Speech

Inspector Lobb took another bite of his salami sandwich.

'Now look here, Mungo,' he said with his mouth full, 'I'll be honest with you. The town's so crammed with crowds of crackpots today that things are a bit disrupted. We've not been able to get back into the museum to find out where you hid that bust, or even whether anything else is missing. So if you could see your way to *telling* us all about this little escapade, and saving us a lot of fuss and bother, then I could quite likely see my way to ordering you another salami sandwich. Maybe even an apple pie as well.'

Mungo's mouth began to water. He was absolutely ravenous. One salami sandwich went nowhere at all in a frame the size of Mungo's, and apple pie was his especial favourite. Besides, the SWAG sack was sure to have been picked up by now. It was probably on its way to being handed in at this very police station at this very moment. So where was the harm in confessing? He needn't say anything about the Eyeball Diamond, of course, and once he got out of here the bust would have been returned to the museum and there would be nothing to stop Mungo having another go at snatch-

46

ing it.

'All right, you win, Inspector!' cried Mungo with seeming reluctance. 'I'll make a full confession.'

At a signal from the Inspector, Constable Dribble perched his notebook on his knee and licked his pencil as Mungo began: 'Hero worship, that was the start of it all. A rare disease these days, but a bad one. Once you suffer from that, you're a lost soul.'

Inspector Lobb's lip began to curl. 'Come off it, Mungo! The day anyone takes you for a hero, I'll eat shredded sweaty socks for breakfast.'

Mungo's eyes grew round with innocent wonder.

'Oh, not me, Inspector. I'm just the humble worshipper. Baron Banks is the hero. You see, I've always admired what he did for this town, and wished I could do half as much myself. Only there's one little snag about giving away a fortune—you have to *have* a fortune to start with. Me, I'm broke. So I thought of this charity stunt, to make money for the Children's Home. I'm sure the Baron wouldn't have minded his bust being borrowed for such a good cause.'

'Well, you do surprise me, Mungo! Are you asking me to believe that you're nothing but a sentimental old idiot after all?'

'Exactly, Inspector!' agreed Mungo, managing to wet his finger and drag it across his cheek like the path of a fallen tear.

Later that night, Constable Dribble was sent along

48

to look for the sack. With Mungo's instructions it did not take him long to find it, despite the weeds. Then he had the pleasure of dragging the Curator back to the museum from a comfortable after-dinner nap, to identify the bust.

The Curator was not pleased. He had spent a draughty day with two missing window-panes, and as a result he now had rheumaticky twinges in his shoulder. Also, the bust was damaged. One of its eyeballs was missing.

'The person responsible for this vandalism will have to pay,' he told Constable Dribble. 'The thing looks ridiculous with only one eye.'

The Constable was bound to agree that it did. Still, the Curator ought to be thankful for small mercies. The whole head could have been kicked to pieces by the mob.

The Constable failed to notice that there was a hole in the bottom of the SWAG sack . . . a hole more than big enough to let an eyeball through.

6
A Thorny Problem

After a totally chaotic meeting, the Mayor and councillors finally reached agreement. Arthur Venger must
spray all the weeds with ALIWOS as fast as possible
and kill them off, in spite of the perfume, which the
Mayor now referred to tearfully as 'a luxury we must
learn to do without'. Herbie Coswell's prophecy had
shaken him to the shoelaces. 'We'll get *our* town
cleared. The rest of the world will have to take care of
itself. Mind you, I'll send a warning telegram to the
Prime Minister.'

'Mention the ALIWOS,' the Town Clerk urged.
'There's still a chance we can make a fortune out of
that.'

'You mean Mr Venger can!' cried Herbie and Kip
together. Arthur himself was still too upset to do more
than wring his hands and moan.

'It's his invention, and if he doesn't want to use it he
doesn't have to.'

'Now, you look here, young laddie,' the Town Clerk
rounded on Herbie sternly, 'I don't know what the
three of you have been up to, but *you* are the ones who
have caused the trouble, so *you* are the ones who are
going to put it right. So you'd better get out there and

51

start spraying before you find yourselves in *real* trouble.'

'We did warn you! We put all those posters up,'
cried Kip. 'You could have stopped this happening if
you hadn't all been so lazy and careless and lackadaisi-
cal.'

'And we're not spraying anything,' retorted Herbie
stoutly, 'until we're sure you're going to pay for it.' He
had recently read *The Pied Piper of Hamelin* and felt he
knew all about cunning, treacherous mayors and cor-
porations.

'Kip, just pass me a sheet of that paper over there.'

Kip selected a page or two of the Mayor's best
headed notepaper, upon which Herbie began to print a
message in bold capitals: WE AGREE TO PAY
ARTHUR VENGER WHATEVER HE SHALL
REASONABLY DEMAND FOR SETTING TO
RIGHTS THE WEED CRISIS IN GRUMPTON.

'Right! Sign that, all of you, one after another, or
Mr Venger won't spray anything at all. Will you, Mr
Venger?'

'Er—no,' squeaked Arthur. Then, taking courage
from Herbie's evident command of the situation, he
said more loudly and firmly, 'No, I jolly well won't!'

'That's the stuff, Mr Venger,' whispered Kip
encouragingly. 'Never let yourself be browbeaten!'

'*And* you!' cried Herbie, spotting a councillor who
was trying to slink from the room without signing. At

last, when he was satisfied with the contract he had drawn up, he folded it carefully, stuffed it inside his shirt and ushered out Kip and Arthur.

'Where's that ALIWOS, then? Better get started right away.'

'It's going to take ages,' moaned Kip. 'Can't we get some help?'

But Herbie insisted they must do it all themselves. He wasn't going to let any Tom, Dick or Harry loose with Mr Venger's sprays, particularly with a fortune at stake.

'We'll manage. Just keep moving, that's the thing. We'll finish the park by teatime.' Arthur, inspired by Herbie's bossy confidence, had now perked up enough to take charge of the operation. He unlocked the boot of his car, which was full of ALIWOS cans, and the spraying began.

So hard did the three of them concentrate that they scarcely noticed the shouts and shufflings of the greedy crowds around them. Luckily, the crowds did not realise that the three were trying to kill off the Litter-wort, or there would probably have been a massacre. Most thought Arthur and the boys must be watering the weeds, or dealing with the greenfly, and they even cheered them on.

They sprayed until it was nearly dark and they were quite worn out. Even then, they had only just finished the park. All those roads and streets and gardens were

still to do. Yet their weariness was as nothing to their horrified dismay as they finally began to realise an awful fact. The ALIWOS did *not* kill the Litterwort after all! On the contrary, wherever they had sprayed, the weed looked and smelled more wonderful than ever, and continued to grow a good deal faster. The whole park was fast becoming a dense, unmanageable jungle.

They couldn't believe it! Everything had depended on the ALIWOS, and it had let them down. Arthur's guilt and remorse returned in double measure.

At last, they went home to Arthur's bungalow in despair.

'What am I going to do?' Arthur sank down dejectedly at the kitchen table, head in hands. 'Not only am I a failure and a laughing-stock, but I've probably ended the world.'

'You must have got it wrong,' pondered Herbie thoughtfully. 'When you made the ALIWOS you must have put in a wrong ingredient or something. Suppose we were to make another lot of ALIWOS and change the proportions?'

'You don't know what you're suggesting!' Arthur wailed. 'There must be about a million permutations. You could go on for ever, and spend a fortune, and still not get it right. It took me five years to come up with this.'

'Well, let's sleep on it. We'll all feel better in the

morning. Herbie and I must go home now, but we'll be back first thing tomorrow to help you again.'

'I wouldn't blame you if you never came near me any more.'

Steeped in self-pity, Arthur gloomily watched his guests depart. Then he slumped down across the table again and wished that he would die. Why was it that whenever he had a wonderful, earth-shattering idea, he had to go and spoil it with a bit of silly carelessness? 'It's a flaw in my character,' the little red-head told himself woefully. 'I really need a couple of assistants to keep a check on me. But nobody would want to work with a failure like me. I wish I'd never been born!'

Ten minutes later the boys were back. There was a great, excited commotion as they rushed in without knocking.

'Mr Venger, Mr Venger, the others are all dead!'

Arthur sat up with a jerk. What did they mean? Was he a mass murderer now? Had the entire population of Grumpton succumbed to the sweet but deadly perfume? No, no; that couldn't be right, or he and the boys would be dead themselves. Then what . . .?

'The other Litterwort—the lot we *didn't* spray with ALIWOS—the stuff in the streets! It's dying off by the ton!'

'It must only last a day or so!'

Arthur sat up even straighter. Then he stood up, whacking the table wildly. 'Wow! Do you realise what

this means?'

'Of course!' replied Herbie promptly. 'It means this isn't the end of civilisation after all, but the start of a wealthy, famous Grumpton.'

'And a wealthy, famous Arthur Venger,' added Kip.

'All that stuff sold at the market will have died, as well. And as the ALIWOS spray seems to keep the Litterwort *alive,* we can have our parkful for as long as we want it.'

'We'll tidy it up a bit, of course.'

'Clear the paths, and so on.'

'Charge admission.'

'Enjoy the perfume ourselves—even up here at the bungalow if the wind's in the right direction.'

'It's a miracle!' Arthur cried at last. 'Do you realise that if I hadn't got it wrong...?'

'Just goes to show,' Kip broke in eagerly, 'that it's an ill wind that has no turning.'

'Of course, I can't expect the Council to pay me now, but never mind.'

'Oh, yes you can! I was very careful how I worded that contract. It didn't say anything about killing off; it only mentioned "setting to rights the weed crisis in Grumpton". Well, you've done that, so they'll have to pay up.'

'Herbie, you're a genius!' cried Kip unnecessarily.

'That was nearly a disaster, though. I think we'd

have been better off with the original Tidy Bags, after all. Tell you what, I'll give that idea a try for a day or two and see what I think of it.'

Herbie plunged his hand inside his shirt to draw forth the famous contract—and discovered that he'd lost it! Somewhere out there it was just another piece of litter.

7
Turning Over a New Leaf

Nobody has bad luck all the time. As if the Fates were determined to console Herbie Coswell for the loss of his contract, it was he who found the Eyeball Diamond as he pushed his broom through heaps of withered Litterwort. By this time, the Eyeball was covered in dirt and it was difficult to tell what it might be. Herbie guessed at a marble, and thought he might clean it up some time and give it to Kip, who collected them. But right now he was busy helping to clear the town. He slipped the Eyeball Diamond into his home-made Tidy Bag and forgot all about it.

Days passed; days in which Arthur and the boys had not time to think of anything but the Litterwort. With the help of Bert Higgs, the Park Superintendent, and his army of gardeners, Grumpton park soon became a tidy place once more. The paths were left unsprayed, then cleared of dead weeds, and everywhere else the Litterwort had been pruned into order. It thrived in shapely flower-beds bordered with tiny coloured stones. It made great archways over gates, and threw up columns and cones of colour among the trees. And over all, the wonderful scent wafted its fan of happiness. Meantime, the refuse carts had been out in the

streets, clearing away the swept-up heaps of dead Litterwort. Paving stones were pushed back into place where spreading roots and shoots had forced them apart. The little town of Grumpton was coming back to life.

Back to a strange new life. For by now, of course, Grumpton's fame had spread across the whole country and beyond. Pictures of it were constantly seen on television news—(all channels). Visitors poured into the place to see—and more importantly, to smell—the Litterwort. Telephones never ceased ringing as long-distance callers tried to book rooms for a night, or a week or a whole summer. House prices soared. New tea rooms opened round every corner, and car parks in every spare bit of field. As far away as California, Grumpton-bound planes were being chartered, while in the depths of the Kremlin special agents were being briefed to sniff out this possibly world-threatening phenomenon. In short, Grumpton was on the map.

Grumptonians grew proud. Almost overnight, they developed a keen sense of loyalty to their hometown which was wonderful to behold. Instead of grumbling about the rotten bus service, the pigeon-droppings on the cenotaph and the lack of things to do on Saturday nights, they began to boast about the number of years they had lived in the place, and how many relatives they had in the local graveyard. They smartened themselves up in case some snooping television camera should catch them unawares; and for the same reason they washed their curtains, painted their front doors, tidied their gardens, mopped their steps and bought new dustbins. The place was practically unrecognisable. And all the time the wonderful perfume from the park filled everyone with joyful energy.

Yet, unlike the residents, the visitors had no pride in Grumpton. They didn't care about the town, except as a place to go for a picnic or a nice day out or a weekend away from work. Most of these visitors ate their lunches in the park, then threw down their empty bottles, tins, bags, packets, paper cups and plastic forks. Not to mention bus tickets, paper hankies, comics, camera-film cartons, toothpicks, disposable nappies, chewing-gum and a million other objects. Grumptonians grew more and more enraged. Here were they, slaving away to make the place look nice, and along came these uneducated louts who strewed their rubbish hither and thither without a moment's thought. It had to stop! (In fact, the Grumptonians began to feel exactly as Arthur Venger had felt when this story first started.)

The number of litter bins in the town was doubled, then trebled, with almost no effect. Great signs were set up, saying: DO NOT LEAVE YOUR LITTER HERE! but unseen vandals merely painted out the 'DO NOT'. At last, in despair, the Mayor called yet another emergency meeting, to which Arthur and his two young cronies were invited.

'Our town,' the Mayor pointed out, 'has become a remarkable place. It's unique. Everybody wants to see it. It's a showpiece, in fact. Well, the one thing about a showpiece is that it must always look its best. Same with princesses and such. You wouldn't want to see a princess with a ladder in her tights and black smudge on her nose and a hole in the elbow of her cardigan.'

'I wouldn't want to see *anybody* like that,' interrupted Herbie Coswell. 'Waitress or auntie or school-dinner-lady or whoever she was.'

'Yes, yes,' snapped the Mayor. 'Don't interrupt, please! You know perfectly well what I mean. It's the same with our town, I was going to say. From now on, our town must always look its best.'

'It was always the same with our town, even before the Litterwort,' boomed the great voice of Baron Banks, newly returned from his world cruise. 'I'll tell you this, I'm fed up with providing fountains and buildings and gardens that just choke up with litter. We shouldn't have had to wait for something like this to happen before we felt a twinge of pride.

'Hear, hear!'

'Rubbish!'

'Nobody asked him to provide his fountains and gardens.'

'Well, that's gratitude for you!'

'He said he didn't *want* any gratitude. Last time he made a speech, he said . . . .'

The Town Clerk rapped on the table with his little hammer.

'Order, order! Those who interrupt this crucial discussion should have proper suggestions to offer.'

'Well, so we have,' cried Herbie, producing his Tidy Bag. 'If everyone carried one of these to put his litter in as he went about his business, then we'd have no problem at all. Mr Venger's been doing it for years.'

'It was the first of his ideas,' agreed Kip. 'If he hadn't realised that people were too jolly lazy to carry Tidy Bags, then he wouldn't have bothered inventing the Litterwort.'

There were shouts of scorn, disgust and disbelief, as Herbie drew back the strings of the little cloth bag he had been carrying for days. The shouts turned to howls of protest as, in order to demonstrate his point, Herbie began to take out the various items of litter, one by one, and lay them on the table. A screwed-up chocolate-wrapper; a burnt potato crisp; the crust off his lunch-time sandwich; a bit of gristle; a lump of bubble-gum; and—what was this? Something smooth and hard in the bottom of the bag, which Herbie now remembered he had not emptied for several days. The smooth, hard object was, of course, the Eyeball Diamond, now cleaned up from its constant rubbing against the side of the Tidy Bag.

At once, Baron Banks recognised the stone with its painted brown eye.

'The Eyeball Diamond! Where did you get that?'

'Diamond? A diamond as big as an eyeball?' Herbie's brain turned cartwheels, taking in this stunning news. Surely it was another miracle, which he must turn to the best advantage in order to prove his point.

'See what I mean?' he crowed. 'I picked that up as a piece of litter when it was dirty and unrecognisable. I had no idea it was a diamond. If my friend Kip here hadn't been a well-known collector of marbles, I'd have left the thing lying in the gutter. The rain would have washed it down a drain into the sewers, and we'd never have seen it again!'

Whereupon Baron Banks had a heart attack and fell down dead.

8
Wreaths and Smiles

It was a wonderful funeral. Everything in Grumpton closed down for the day, and every inhabitant, not to mention thousands of strangers, thronged the streets to watch the funeral procession. There were flowers galore, including a great cross of Litterwort from Arthur Venger, Kip and Herbie. There was a band playing solemn music all day, and black ribbons streamed from the top of every lamp-post. It would be true to say that the whole occasion was far more spectacular than the Carnival had been, and the *Grumpton Argus* gave it a full front-page spread, with double black border. The vicar, in his funeral oration, spoke of 'this town's great benefactor', and there was scarcely an eye that did not shed a tear.

But after the funeral came the reading of the will. And after the reading of the will came the public declaration that as Herbie Coswell, a true Grumptonian, had genuinely found the Eyeball Diamond, he should be allowed to keep it. That would seem to be what the Baron had intended. Herbie nobly refused to do anything of the kind.

'After all, it was me that killed the poor old Baron, giving him a shock like that. So I can hardly take his valuables.' No amount of reassurance by the Baron's doctor that the Baron had had a bad heart, and could have dropped dead at any moment, made the slightest difference. Herbie would not change his mind.

'What I *will* do,' said Herbie after careful thought, 'is to donate the proceeds from the sale of this diamond to a worthy cause. And the worthiest cause I can think of is the cause of progress towards a better world. Nobody I know has done more research towards that end than my friend, Mr Arthur Venger, who is always looking for cures for the ills of civilisation.' (Herbie saw this as his great chance to make up to Arthur for having lost that contract.) 'Of course, there will be donations, too, to our local charities, such as the Children's Home.'

There were great shouts and cheers among all who heard. (All except Mungo Slye, out on bail pending his trial for breaking and entering at Grumpton Museum.) Those who had felt jealous of Herbie's luck now gave him their ungrudging admiration, and Arthur Venger found himself a sudden hero. As for Perce O'Deary, no one had ever connected him with Mungo's crime, and as he didn't even know it was a crime he hadn't even a guilty conscience. In fact, he thought all this latest talk of money for the Children's Home was what Mungo had been arranging in the first place. Perce felt utterly happy, and quite proud of himself for having helped.

The reporter from the *Grumpton Argus* cornered

Arthur Venger to ask what sort of research could now be undertaken. Arthur's bright blue eyes began to twinkle. All his confidence had returned, and inspiration oozed from every pore. 'How about a Bore-Silencer?' he suggested, looking the reporter straight in the eye, 'to put an instant stop to all those people who ramble on and on about nothing . . . .'

'Including anyone who says, "I told you so!"' Kip amended gleefully.

'Or what about a Politeness Pill?' added Herbie.

'Or a Greed-Dissolver?' Kip went on.

'Or a Bad-Temper-Sweetener?'

'Or a Vanity-Watcher's mirror?'

'Or a . . . .'

'But of course,' declared Arthur as the list of suggestions grew, 'before I could undertake so much work I'd need an increase in staff. A couple of young assistants, say.'

Herbie looked at Kip, and Kip stared back at Herbie, who finally shook his head. 'It's no use. We're stuck with school for the next few centuries.'

Kip looked totally cast down, until Arthur Venger grinned and continued: 'Just evenings, weekends and holidays for a start, until the business really blossoms out in a few years' time. I'll tell you what, boys, if you're not doing anything tomorrow morning . . . .'

Other great reads 🦊 *from* **Red Fox**

Further Red Fox titles that you might enjoy reading are listed on the following pages. They are available in bookshops or they can be ordered directly from us.

   If you would like to order books, please send this form and the money due to:

ARROW BOOKS, BOOKSERVICE BY POST, PO BOX 29, DOUGLAS, ISLE OF MAN, BRITISH ISLES. Please enclose a cheque or postal order made out to Arrow Books Ltd for the amount due, plus 30p per book for postage and packing to a maximum of £3.00, both for orders within the UK. For customers outside the UK, please allow 35p per book.

NAME _____

ADDRESS _____

_____

Please print clearly.

Whilst every effort is made to keep prices low, it is sometimes necessary to increase cover prices at short notice. If you are ordering books by post, to save delay it is advisable to phone to confirm the correct price. The number to ring is THE SALES DEPARTMENT 071 (if outside London) 973 9700.

*Other great reads from **Red Fox***

THE SNIFF STORIES Ian Whybrow

Things just keep happening to Ben Moore. It's dead hard
avoiding disaster when you've got to keep your street cred with
your mates *and* cope with a family of oddballs at the same time.
There's his appalling 2½ year old sister, his scatty parents who
are into healthy eating and animal rights and, worse than all
of these, there's Sniff! If only Ben could just get on with his
scientific experiments and his attempt at a world beating
Swampbeast score . . . but there's no chance of that while chaos
is just around the corner.

ISBN 0 09 975040 6   £2.99

J.B. SUPERSLEUTH Joan Davenport

James Bond is a small thirteen-year-old with spots and
spectacles. But with a name like that, how can he help being
a supersleuth?

It all started when James and 'Polly' (Paul) Perkins spotted
a teacher's stolen car. After that, more and more mysteries
needed solving. With the case of the Arabian prince, the
Murdered Model, the Bonfire Night Murder and the Lost
Umbrella, JB's reputation at Moorside Comprehensive soars.

But some of the cases aren't quite what they seem . . .

ISBN 0 09 971780 8   £2.99

Other great reads from Red Fox

Discover the great animal stories of Colin Dann

JUST NUFFIN

The Summer holidays loomed ahead with nothing to look forward to except one dreary week in a caravan with only Mum and Dad for company. Roger was sure he'd be bored.

But then Dad finds Nuffin: an abandoned puppy who's more a bundle of skin and bones than a dog. Roger's holiday is transformed and he and Nuffin are inseparable. But Dad is adamant that Nuffin must find a new home. Is there *any* way Roger can persuade him to change his mind?

ISBN 0 09 966900 5   £2.99

KING OF THE VAGABONDS

'You're very young,' Sammy's mother said, 'so heed my advice. Don't go into Quartermile Field.'

His mother and sister are happily domesticated but Sammy, the tabby cat, feels different. They are content with their lot, never wondering what lies beyond their immediate surroundings. But Sammy is burningly curious and his life seems full of mysteries. Who is his father? Where has he gone? And what is the mystery of Quartermile Field?

ISBN 0 09 957190 0   £2.99

Other great reads from **Red Fox**

School stories from Enid Blyton

THE NAUGHTIEST GIRL IN THE SCHOOL

'Mummy, if you send me away to school, I shall be so naughty there, they'll have to send me back home again,' said Elizabeth. And when her parents won't be budged, Elizabeth sets out to do just that—she stirs up trouble all around her and gets the name of the bold bad schoolgirl. She's sure she's longing to go home—but to her surprise there are some things she hadn't reckoned with. Like making friends . . .

ISBN 0 09 945500 5   £2.99

THE NAUGHTIEST GIRL IS A MONITOR

'Oh dear, I wish I wasn't a monitor! I wish I could go to a monitor for help! I can't even think what I ought to do!'

When Elizabeth Allen is chosen to be a monitor in her third term at Whyteleafe School, she tries to do her best. But somehow things go wrong and soon she is in just as much trouble as she was in her first term, when she was the naughtiest girl in the school!

ISBN 0 09 945490 4   £2.99

Other great reads *from* **Red Fox**

**The latest and funniest joke books are from
Red Fox!**

THE OZONE FRIENDLY JOKE BOOK
Kim Harris, Chris Langham, Robert Lee,
Richard Turner

What's green and highly dangerous?
How do you start a row between conservationists?
What's green and can't be rubbed out?

Green jokes for green people (non-greens will be pea-green
when they see how hard you're laughing), bags and bags of them
(biodegradable of course).

All the jokes in this book are printed on environmentally
friendly paper and every copy you buy will help GREENPEACE
save our planet.

* David Bellamy with a machine gun.
* Pour oil on troubled waters.
* The Indelible hulk.

ISBN 0 09 973190 8 £1.99

THE HAUNTED HOUSE JOKE BOOK
John Hegarty

There are skeletons in the scullery . . .
Beasties in the bath . . .
There are spooks in the sitting room
And jokes to make you laugh . . .

Search your home and see if we are right. Then come back,
sit down and shudder to the hauntingly funny and eerily rib-
rattling jokes in this book.

ISBN 0 09 9621509 £1.99

Other great reads from **Red Fox**

Discover the Red Fox poetry collections

CADBURY'S NINTH BOOK OF CHILDREN'S POETRY
Poems by children aged 4–16.
ISBN 0 09 983450 2   £4.99

THE COMPLETE SCHOOL VERSE
ed. Jennifer Curry
Two books in one all about school.
ISBN 0 09 991790 4   £2.99

MY NAME, MY POEM ed. Jennifer Curry
Find *your* name in this book.
ISBN 0 09 948030 1   £1.95

MONSTROSITIES Charles Fuge
Grim, gruesome poems about monsters.
ISBN 0 09 967330 4   £3.50

LOVE SHOUTS AND WHISPERS Vernon Scannell
Read about all sorts of love in this book.
ISBN 0 09 973950 X   £2.99

CATERPILLAR STEW Gavin Ewart
A collection describing all sorts of unusual animals.
ISBN 0 09 967280 4   £2.50

HYSTERICALLY HISTORICAL Gordon Snell and Wendy Shea
Madcap rhymes from olden times
ISBN 0 09 972160 0   £2.99